Shadow

By
I. T. Thurston

The Bishop's Shadow

I. LOST--A POCKETBOOK

It was about ten o'clock in the morning and a northeast storm was raging in Boston.

The narrow crooked business streets were slippery with mud and thronged with drays and wagons of every description, which, with the continual passing of the street cars, made it a difficult and often a dangerous matter to attempt a crossing.

The rain came in sudden driving sheets, blotting out all but the nearest cars or vehicles, while the wind seemed to lie in wait at every corner ready to spring forth and wrest umbrellas out of the hands of pedestrians at the most critical points in the crossings.

Two ladies coming along Causeway street by the Union Depot, waited some minutes on the sidewalk watching for an opening in the endless stream of passing teams.

"There! We shan't have a better chance than this. Come on now," one of them exclaimed, stepping quickly forward as there came a little break in the moving line. She stepped in front of two cars that had stopped on parallel tracks and her companion hastily followed her. Just then there came a fierce gust that threatened to turn their umbrellas inside out. The lady in front clutched hers nervously and hurried forward. As she ran past the second car she found herself almost under the feet of a pair of horses attached to a heavy wagon. The driver yelled angrily at her as he hastily pulled up his team; a policeman shouted warningly and sprang toward her, and her friend stopped short with a low cry of terror. But though the pole of the wagon grazed her cheek and the shock threw her almost to the ground, the lady recovered herself and hurried across to the sidewalk.

It was then that a little ragged fellow of perhaps thirteen, slipped swiftly under the very feet of the horses, and, unheeding the savage shouts of the driver, wormed his way rapidly through the crowd and vanished. As he did so, the lady who had so narrowly escaped injury, turned to her friend and cried,

"Oh my pocketbook! I must have dropped it on the crossing."

"On the crossing, did you say?" questioned the policeman, and as she assented, he turned hastily back to the street, but the cars and teams had passed on and others were surging forward and no trace of the pocketbook was visible. The policeman came back and questioned the lady about it, promising to do what he could to recover it.

"But it's not probable you'll ever see a penny of the money again," he said. "Some rascally thief most likely saw ye drop it an' snatched it up."

The policeman was not mistaken. If he had turned through Tremont and Boylston streets he might have seen a ragged, barefooted boy sauntering along with his hands in his pockets, stopping now and then to look into a shop window, yet ever keeping a keenly watchful eye on every policeman he met. The boy looked as if he had not a penny in those ragged pockets of his, but one of his grimy hands clutched tightly the lost pocketbook, which his sharp eyes had seen as it fell beneath the feet of the horses, and which he had deftly appropriated as he wriggled through the mud.

Heedless of wind and rain the boy lounged along the street. It was not often that he found himself in this section of the city, and it was much less familiar to him than some other localities. He seemed to be wandering aimlessly along, but his restless eyes were on the watch for some retired spot where he might safely examine his prize and see how much money he had secured. For a long time he saw no place that seemed to him a safe one for his purpose, so he went on and on until suddenly he realised that he was tired. He was passing a large brownstone church at the moment, and he sat down on the steps to rest.

"My! But this is a gay ol' church!" he thought, as he looked curiously at the beautiful building. "Wonder where them steps go to."

Springing up he ran across the pillared porch to the foot of the stone stairs that led to the upper entrance to the chapel. Following a sudden impulse he started hastily up these stairs, his bare feet making no sound. At the top of the stairs he found himself shut in on two sides by a high stone balustrade, the chapel door forming the third side. This door was closed. He tried it softly and found it locked. Then he dropped down in the darkest corner of the landing, and, with eyes and ears still keenly alert, pulled from his pocket the mud-stained purse and examined it carefully. He found in it thirty-six dollars in bills and about a dollar more in silver.

The boy gave a gleeful, silent laugh. "Struck it rich this time," he said to himself.

He hunted up a crooked pin from somewhere about his dilapidated garments, and fastened the roll of bills as securely as he could inside the lining of his jacket, keeping the silver in his pocket. Then he again examined the book to be sure that he had overlooked nothing. On the inside of the leather was the name,

"R. A. RUSSELL,"

and there was also a card bearing the same name and an address. The card he tore into tiny bits and chewed into a pellet which he tossed over the stone balustrade. Then, with the pocketbook in his hand, he looked about him. There was a pastor's box fastened beside the door. He crowded the telltale book through the opening in the top of this box, and then with a satisfied air ran blithely down the stone steps. But he stopped short as he came face to face with the sexton who was just crossing the porch.

"Here, you! Where've you been? What you been up to?" cried the man, clutching at him angrily, but the boy was too quick.

He ducked suddenly, slipped under the sexton's hands and darted across the porch and down the steps. Then he stopped to call back,

"Be'n makin' 'rangements ter preach fer ye here next Sunday--yah! yah!" and with a mocking laugh he disappeared leaving the sexton shaking his fist in impotent wrath.

The boy ran swiftly on until he had gotten quite a distance from the church; then he slackened his pace and began to plan what he should do next. The sight of a confectioner's window reminded him that he was hungry, and he went into the store and bought two tarts which he ate as he walked on. After that he bought a quart of peanuts, two bananas and a piece of mince-pie, and having disposed of all these he felt hungry no longer.

Having in his possession what seemed to him a small fortune, he saw no necessity for working, so that night he did not go as usual to the newspaper office for the evening papers, but spent his time loafing around the busiest corners and watching all that went on about the streets. This unusual conduct attracted the attention of his cronies, and a number of newsboys gathered about him trying to find out the reason of his strange idleness.

"I say, Tode," called one, "why ain't ye gettin' yer papers?"

"Aw, he's come into a fortune, he has," put in another. "His rich uncle's come home an' 'dopted him."

"Naw, he's married Vanderbilt's daughter," sneered a third.

"Say, now, Tode, tell us w'at's up," whispered one, sidling up to him. "Hev ye swiped somethin'?"

Tode tried to put on an expression of injured innocence, but his face flushed as he answered, shortly,

"Come, hush yer noise, will ye! Can't a chap lay off fer one day 'thout all the town pitchin' inter him? I made a dollar extry this mornin'--that's all the' is about it," and stuffing his hands into his pockets he marched off to avoid further comment.

For the next week Tode "lived high" as he expressed it. He had from three to six meals a day and an unlimited amount of pie and peanuts besides, but after all he was not particularly happy. Time hung heavy on his hands sometimes--the more so as the boys, resenting his living in luxurious idleness, held aloof, and would have nothing to do with him. He had been quite a leader among them, and it galled him to be so left out and ignored. He began to think that he should not be sorry when his ill-gotten money was gone. He was thinking after this fashion one day as he strolled aimlessly down a side street. It was a quiet street where at that hour there was little passing, and Tode lounged along with his hands in his pockets until he came to a place where the sidewalk was littered with building material and where a large house was in course of construction. Perhaps the workmen were on a strike that day. At any rate none of them were about, and the boy sprang up onto a barrel that was standing near the curbstone, and sat there drumming on the head with two pieces of lath and whistling a lively air.

After a little his whistle ceased and he looked up and down the street with a yawn, saying to himself,

"Gay ol' street, this is! Looks like everybody's dead or asleep."

But even as he spoke a girl came hastily around the nearest corner and hurried toward him. She looked about fourteen. Her clothes were worn and shabby but they were clean, and in her arms she carried a baby wrapped in a shawl. She stopped beside Tode and looked at him with imploring eyes.

"Oh can't you help me to hide somewhere? Do! Do!" she cried, with a world of entreaty in her voice.

The boy glanced at her coolly.

"What ye want ter hide for? Been swipin' somethin'?" he questioned, carelessly.

The girl flashed at him an indignant glance, then cast a quick, frightened one behind her.

"No, no!" she exclaimed, earnestly. "I'm no thief. I'm running away from old Mary Leary. She's most killed my little brother giving him whiskey so's to make him look sick when she takes him out begging. Look here!"

She lifted the shawl that was wrapped about the child. Tode leaned over and looked at the little face. It was a pitiful little face--so white and thin, with sunken eyes and blue lips--so pitiful that it touched even Tode's heart, that was not easily touched.

"The ol' woman after ye?" he asked, springing down from the barrel.

"Yes, yes! Oh, do help me," pleaded the girl, the tears running down her cheeks as she gazed at the baby face. "I'm afraid he's going to die."

The boy cast a quick glance about him.

"Here!" he exclaimed, "squat down an' I'll turn this over ye."

He seized a big empty barrel that stood near. Without a word the girl slipped to the ground and he turned the barrel over her, kicking under the edge a bit of wood to give air. The next moment he stooped down to the opening and whispered,

"Hi! The ol' lady's a comin'. Don't ye peep. I'll fix her!"

Then he reseated himself again on the barrelhead and began to drum and whistle as before, apparently paying no heed to the woman who came along scolding and swearing, with half a dozen street children following at her heels. She came nearer and nearer but Tode drummed on and whistled unconcernedly until she stopped before him and exclaimed harshly,

"You boy--have you seen a girl go by here, with a baby?"

"Nope," replied Tode, briefly.

"How long you be'n settin' here?"

"'Bout two weeks," answered the boy, gravely.

7

The woman stormed and blustered, but finding that this made no impression she changed her tactics and began in a wheedling tone,

"Now, dearie, you'll help an ol' woman find her baby, won't ye? It's heartbroke I am for my pretty darlin' an' that girl has carried him off. Tell me, dearie, did they go this way?"

"I d' know nothin' 'bout yer gal," exclaimed Tode. "Why don't ye scoot 'round an' find her 'f she's cleared out?"

"An' ain't I huntin' her this blessed minute?" shrieked the woman, angrily. "I b'lieve ye have seen her. Like's not ye've hid her away somewheres."

Tode turned away from her and resumed his drumming while the woman cast a suspicious glance at the unfinished building.

"She may be there," she muttered and began searching through the piles of building material on the ground floor.

"Hope she'll break her ol' neck!" thought Tode, vengefully, as he whistled with fresh vigor.

The woman reappeared presently, and casting a threatening glance and a torrent of bad language at the boy, went lumbering heavily down the street with the crowd of noisy, curious children straggling along behind her.

When they had all disappeared around the corner of the street, Tode sprang down and putting his mouth to the opening at the bottom of the barrel whispered hastily,

"Keep still 'til I see if she's gone sure," and he raced up to the corner where he watched until the woman was out of sight. Then he ran back and lifted the barrel off, saying,

"It's all right--she's gone, sure 'nough."

The girl cast an anxious glance up and down the street as she sprang up.

"Oh dear!" she exclaimed. "I don't know where to go!" and Tode saw that her eyes were full of tears.

8

He looked at her curiously.

"Might go down t' the wharf. Ol' woman wouldn't be likely ter go there, would she?" he suggested.

"I don't think so. I've never been there," replied the girl. "Which way is it?"

"Come on--I'll show ye;" and Tode set off at a rapid pace.

The girl followed as fast as she could, but the child was a limp weight in her arms and she soon began to lag behind and breathe heavily. "What's the matter? Why don't ye hurry up?" exclaimed the boy with an impatient backward glance.

"I--can't. He's so--heavy," panted the girl breathlessly.

Tode did not offer to take the child. He only put his hands in his pockets and waited for her, and then went on more slowly.

When they reached the wharf, he led the way to a quiet corner where the girl dropped down with a sigh of relief and weariness, while he leaned against a post and looked down at her. Presently he remarked,

"What's yer name?" "Nan Hastings," replied the girl.

"How'd she get hold o' ye?" pursued the boy, with a backward jerk of his thumb that Nan rightly concluded was meant to indicate the Leary woman.

She answered slowly, "It was when mother died. We had a nice home. We were not poor folks. My father was an engineer, and he was killed in an accident before Little Brother was born, and that almost broke mother's heart. After the baby came she was sick all the time and she couldn't work much, and so we used up all the money we had, and mother got sicker and at last she told me she was going to die." The girl's voice trembled and she was silent for a moment; then she went on, "She made me kneel down by the bed and promise her that I would always take care of Little Brother and bring him up to be a good man as father was. I promised, and I am going to do it."

The girl spoke earnestly with the light of a solemn purpose in her dark eyes.

Tode began to be interested. "And she died?" he prompted.

"Yes, she died. She wrote to some of her relatives before she died asking them to help Little Brother and me, but there was no answer to the letter, and after she died all our furniture was sold to pay the doctor and the funeral bills. The doctor wanted to send us to an orphan asylum, but Mary Leary had worked for us, and she told me that if we went to an asylum they would take Little Brother away from me and I'd never see him any more, and she said if I'd go home with her she'd find me a place to work and I could keep the baby. So I went home with her. It was a horrid place"-- Nan shuddered--"and I found out pretty soon that she drank whiskey, but I hadn't any other place to go, so I had to stay there, but lately she's been taking the baby out every day and he's been growing so pale and sick-looking, and yesterday I caught her giving him whiskey, and then I knew she did it to make him look sick so that she would get more money when she went out begging with him."

"An' so you cut an' run?" put in Tode, as the girl paused.

"Yes--and I'll never go back to her, but--I don't know what I can do. Do you know any place where I can stay and work for Little Brother?"

The dark eyes looked up into the boy's face with a wistful, pleading glance, as the girl spoke.

"I'd know no place," replied Tode, shrugging his shoulders carelessly. He did not feel called upon to help this girl. Tode considered girls entirely unnecessary evils.

Nan looked disappointed, but she said no more.

"He's wakin' up, I guess," remarked Tode, glancing at the baby.

The little thing stirred uneasily, and then the heavy, blue-veined lids were lifted slowly, and a pair of big innocent blue eyes looked straight into

10

Tode's. A long, steadfast, unchildlike look it was, a look that somehow held the boy's eyes in spite of himself, and then a faint, tremulous smile quivered over the pale lips, and the baby hands were lifted to the boy.

That look and smile had a strange, a wonderful effect on Tode. Something seemed to spring into life in his heart in that instant. Up to this hour he had never known what love was, for he had never loved any human being, but as he gazed into the pure depths of those blue eyes and saw the baby fingers flutter feebly toward him, his heart went out in love to the child, and he held out his arms to take him.

Nan hesitated, with a quick glance at Tode's dirty hands and garments, but he cried imperiously,

"Give him here. He wants to come to me," and she allowed him to take the child from her arms. As he felt himself lifted in that strong grasp, Little Brother smiled again, and nestled with a long breath of content against Tode's dirty jacket.

"See--he likes me!" cried the boy, his face all aglow with the strange, sweet delight that possessed him. He sat still holding the child, afraid to move lest he disturb his charge, but in a few minutes the baby began to fret.

"What's he want?" questioned Tode, anxiously.

Nan looked distressed. "I'm afraid he's hungry," she replied. "Oh dear, what shall I do!"

She seemed ready to cry herself, but Tode sprang up.

"You come along," he exclaimed, briefly, and he started off with the child still in his arms, and Nan followed wonderingly. She shrank back as he pushed open the door of a restaurant, but Tode went in and after a moment's hesitation, she followed.

"What'll he take--some beef?" inquired the boy.

"Oh no!" cried Nan, hastily, "some bread and milk will be best for him."

11

"All right. Here you--bring us a quart o' milk an' a loaf o' bread," called Tode, sharply, to a waiter.

When these were brought he added, "Now fetch on a steak an' a oyster stew."

Then he turned with a puzzled look to Nan. "How does he take it? D'ye pour it down his throat?" he asked.

"No, no!" cried Nan, hastily, as he seized the bowl of milk. "You must feed it to him with a spoon."

"All right!" and utterly regardless of the grinning waiters Tode began to feed the baby, depositing quite as much in his neck as in his mouth, while Nan looked on, longing to take the matter into her own hands, but afraid to interfere. Suddenly Tode glanced at her.

"Why don't ye eat?" he said, with a gesture toward the food on the table. The girl coloured and drew back.

"Oh I can't," she exclaimed, hastily, "I ain't--I don't want anything."

"Ain't ye hungry?" demanded Tode in a masterful tone.

"N--not much," stammered Nan, but the boy saw a hungry gleam in her eyes as she glanced at the food.

"Y'are, too! Now you jest put that out o' sight in a hurry!"

But Nan shook her head. "I'm no beggar," she said, proudly, "and some time I'm going to pay you for that," and she pointed to the bowl of bread and milk.

"Shucks!" exclaimed the boy. "See here! I've ordered that stuff an' I'll have it to pay for anyhow, so you might's well eat it. I don't want it," and he devoted himself again to the child.

Nan turned her head resolutely away, but she was so hungry and the food did smell so good that she could not resist it. She tasted the oysters and in three minutes the bowl was empty, and a good bit of the steak had disappeared before she pushed aside her plate.

"Thank you," she said, gratefully. "It did taste so good!"

"Huh!" grunted Tode. This was the first time in his life that anybody had said "thank you" to him.

He handed the baby over to Nan and, though he had said he was not hungry, finished the steak and a big piece of pie in addition and then the three left the restaurant.

II. NAN'S NEW HOME

As they went out, Nan looked anxiously from side to side, fearing to see or be seen by the Leary woman. Tode noticed her troubled look and remarked,

"Ye needn't ter fret. I wouldn't let her touch ye. We might's well go back to the wharf," he added.

So they returned to the corner they had left, and in a little while the baby dropped into a refreshing sleep in his sister's lap, while Tode sometimes roamed about the wharf, and sometimes lounged against a post and talked with Nan.

"What is your name?" she asked him, suddenly.

"Tode Bryan."

"Tode? That's a queer name."

"'Spect that ain't all of it. There's some more, but I've forgot what 'tis," the boy replied, carelessly.

"And where's your home, Tode?"

"Home? Ain't got none. Never had none--no folks neither."

"But where do you live?"

"Oh, anywheres. When I'm flush, I sleeps at the Newsboys' Home, an' when I ain't, I takes the softest corner I can find in a alley or on a doorstep," was the indifferent reply.

Nan looked troubled.

"But I can't do that," she said. "I can't sleep in the street with Little Brother."

"Why not?" questioned Tode, wonderingly.

"Oh because--girls can't do like that."

"Lots o' girls do."

"But--not nice girls, Tode," said Nan, wistfully.

"Well no, I don't 'spect they're nice girls. I don't know any girls 't amount to much," replied Tode, disdainfully.

Nan flushed at his tone, as she answered,

"But what can I do? Where can I go? Seems as if there ought to be some place where girls like me could stay."

"That's so, for a fact," assented Tode, then he added, thoughtfully, "The's one feller--mebbe you could stay where he lives. He's got a mother, I know."

"Oh if I only could, Tode! I'd work ever so hard," said Nan, earnestly.

"You stay here an' I'll see 'f I can find him," said the boy. Then he turned back to add suspiciously, "Now don't ye clear out while I'm gone."

Nan looked at him wonderingly.

"Where would I go?" she questioned, and Tode answered with a laugh,

"That a fact--ye ain't got no place to go, have ye?"

Then he disappeared and Nan waited anxiously for his return. He came back within an hour bringing with him a freckle-faced boy a year or so older than himself.

"This's the gal!" he remarked, briefly.

The newcomer looked doubtfully at Nan.

"See the little feller," cried Tode, eagerly. "Ain't he a daisy? See him laugh," and he chucked the baby clumsily under the chin.

The child's heavy eyes brightened and he smiled back into the friendly, dirty face of the boy.

The other boy looked at Tode wonderingly. "Didn't know 't you liked kids," he said, scornfully.

"So I don't--but this one's diff'runt," replied Tode, promptly. "You ain't no common kid, be ye, Little Brother?"

"What's his name?" questioned the boy.

"His name is David, but mother always called him Little Brother, and so I do," answered the girl, in a low tone. "Have you a mother?" she added, with an earnest look at the boy.

"Got the best mother in this town," was the prompt reply.

"Oh, won't you take me to her, then? Maybe she can tell me what to do," Nan pleaded.

"Well, come along, then," responded the boy, rather grudgingly.

"You come too, Tode," said Nan. "'Cause you know we might meet Mary Leary."

"All right. I'll settle her. Don't you worry," and Tode, with a very warlike air marched along at Nan's right hand.

"What's your mother's name?" questioned Nan, shyly, of the newcomer as the three walked on together.

"Hunt. I'm Dick Hunt," was the brief reply. Then Dick turned away from the girl and talked to Tode.

It was not very far to Dick's home. It was in one of the better class of tenement houses. The Hunts had three rooms and they were clean and comfortably furnished. Tode looked around admiringly as Dick threw open the door and led the way in. Tode had never been in rooms like these before. Nan--after one quick glance about the place--looked earnestly and longingly into Mrs. Hunt's kind motherly face. Dick wasted no words.

"Mother," he said, "this girl wants to stay here."

Mrs. Hunt was making paper bags. Her busy fingers did not stop for a moment, but she cast a quick, keen glance at Nan and Tode.

"What do you mean, Dick?" she said.

"Oh, Mrs. Hunt, if you only would let us stay here till I can find a place to work, I'd be so thankful. We'll have to stay in the street tonight--Little Brother and I--if you don't," urged Nan, eagerly.

Mrs. Hunt's kind heart was touched by the girl's pleading tone. She had girls of her own and she thought, "What if my Nellie had to spend the night in the street," but she said only:

"Sit down, my dear, and tell me all about it."

The kind tone and those two words "my dear," were almost too much for poor anxious Nan. Her eyes filled with tears and her voice was not quite steady as she told again her sorrowful little story, and when it was ended the mother's eyes too were dim.

"Give me that baby," she exclaimed, forgetting her work for the moment, and she took the little fellow tenderly in her arms. "You poor child," she added, to Nan, "of course you can stay here to-night. It's a poor enough place an' we're as pinched as we can be, but we'll manage somehow to squeeze out a bite and a corner for you for a day or two anyway."

Tode's face expressed his satisfaction as he turned to depart. Dick too looked pleased.

"Didn't I tell ye I'd got the best mother in this town?" he said, proudly, as he followed Tode down the stairs.

"Yes you did, an' 'twarn't no lie neither," assented Tode, emphatically; "but, see here, you can tell your mother that I'm agoin' to pay for that little feller's bread an' milk."

Dick looked at him curiously.

"You goin' to work again?" he questioned.

"'Course I am."

"Somebody's got your beat."

"Who?" Tode stopped short in angry surprise as he asked the question.

"That big red-headed feller that they call Carrots."

"Well--Carrots'll find himself knocked out o' business," declared Tode, fiercely.

When the newsboys assembled at the newspaper office a little later, Dick speedily reported Tode's remark, and soon all eyes were on the alert to see what would happen. Tode was greeted rather coldly and indifferently, but that did not trouble him. He bought his papers and set off for his usual beat. Scenting a fight a good many of the boys followed. As Dick had said, Tode found the big fellow on the ground, lustily crying his papers. Tode marched straight up to him.

"See here, Carrots, this's my beat. You clear out--d'ye hear?" he shouted.

The big fellow leered at him scornfully, and without a word in response, went on calling his papers.

Down on the ground went Tode's stock in trade, and he fell upon Carrots like a small cyclone fighting with teeth, nails, fists and heels, striking in recklessly with never a thought of fear.

Forgetful of possible customers, the boys quickly formed a ring, and yelled and hooted at the antagonists, cheering first one and then the other. But the contest was an unequal one. The red-headed boy was the bigger and stronger of the two and plucky as Tode was, he would have been severely treated had not the affair been ended by the appearance of a policeman who speedily separated the combatants.

"What's all this row about?" he demanded, sharply, as he looked from Tode's bleeding face to the big fellow's bruised eye.

"He took my beat. I've sold papers here for three years," cried Tode, angrily.

"What you got to say?" The policeman turned to the other.

"He give it up. He ain't sold a paper here for a week past," growled Carrots.

"Whose beat is it?" The man turned to the other boys as he asked the question.

"Reckon it's Tode's."

"He's o'ny been layin' off fer a spell."

"It's Tode's sure 'nough."

So they answered, and the officer turned again to Carrots.

"You're a bigger feller 'n he is. You let him alone an' go find a new beat for yourself, an' see 't I don't catch either of ye fightin' in the streets again, or I'll put ye where ye'll get another kind of a beat if ye don't walk straight. Now scatter--all of ye!"

The "fun" was over and the boys needed no second bidding. They scattered in all directions and the next moment, Tode's shrill voice rang out triumphantly, while his rival stalked gloomily off, meditating dire vengeance in the near future.

Meantime, after Tode and Dick had departed, Nan had spoken a few grateful words to Mrs. Hunt, and then laying the baby on the lounge, she said, earnestly,

"Please show me just how you make those bags. I'm sure I can do it."

It was simple work and it did not take her many minutes to master the details. Her quick eyes and deft fingers soon enabled her to do the work fully as well and as rapidly as Mrs. Hunt could do it.

"Well, I never! You certainly are a quick one," exclaimed the good woman as she gave up her seat to the girl. "Now if you can finish that job for me, I can get a little sewing done before dark."

"Oh yes, I can finish this easily," exclaimed Nan, delighted that there was something that she could do in return for the kindness shown her.

By and by, Jimmy, Nellie, and the younger children came in from school, staring in amazement at the two strangers who seemed so much at home there. Nan made friends with them at once, but she dreaded the arrival of the father.

"What if he shouldn't want us to stay?" she thought, anxiously, as she heard a heavy step on the stairs, and Nellie called out,

"Here comes father!"

There was a general rush of the children as he opened the door and he came into the room with boys and girls swarming over him. Nan's fears departed at the first sight of his honest, kindly face, and his cheery greeting to her.

"Wal' now, this is nice," he said, heartily, after hearing his wife's brief explanation. "Never can have too many little gals 'round to suit me, an' as fer this young man," he lifted Little Brother gently as he spoke, "he fits into this fam'ly jest like a book. Ted here's gettin' most too much of a man to be our baby any longer."

Ted's round face had lengthened as his father took up the baby, but it brightened at these words, and he straightened himself and slipped his hands into the pockets of the very short trousers he was wearing.

"I'll be a big man pretty soon," he remarked, and his father patted his head tenderly as he answered,

"So you will, sonny, so you will, an' the more you help other folks the faster you'll grow."

That was a happy evening for Nan. As she sat at the supper-table at "father's" right hand the only shadow on her satisfaction was the fear that she might not be allowed to remain in this friendly household. But somehow, even that thought could not cast a very dark shadow on her heart when she looked up into the sunshine of Father Hunt's plain face, or met the motherly smile of his good wife. She lent a helping hand whenever she saw an opportunity to do so, and the table was cleared, and the dishes washed so quickly that Mr. Hunt remarked to his wife,

"Look here, now, mother, why can't you an' me go somewheres this evening? You ain't been out with me for more'n a year, an' I feel's if I'd like a bit of an outin' to-night."

Mrs. Hunt looked up doubtfully, but Nan spoke up quickly,

"Do go, Mrs. Hunt. I'll take care of the children and be glad to."

"That's right! That's right!" exclaimed Mr. Hunt. "'Course ye will, an' I 'spect you'll make 'em have such a fine time that they'll be sorry when we get back."

Ted put his finger in his mouth and gloom gathered on his round face at this suggestion, but it vanished as Nan said,

"Teddy, I can cut fine soldiers out of paper, and animals too. After your father and mother go I'll cut some for you."

Teddy's face brightened at this promise, and he saw the door close behind his mother without shedding a single tear.

Nan put Little Brother to bed and then all the children gathered about the table and Nan drew men and animals on brown paper and cut them out, to the great delight of the children. Teddy especially was so interested that once Nellie remarked, "You needn't get quite into Nan's mouth, Ted."

Nan laughed. "If he only won't get his fingers cut instead of the paper," she said.

"There! I've got a whole fun'ral of horses," remarked Ted, in a tone of great satisfaction, as he ranged a long string of the figures two and two on the table.

"Look out, Ted, you'll knock over the lamp!" cried Jimmy, hastily.

The warning came too late. Even as the words were uttered, the chair on which Ted was standing slipped from under him, and as he struck out wildly to save himself from falling he hit the lamp and knocked it over on the table. The chimney rolled to the floor with a crash, and the burning oil spread over the table licking up Ted's horses and the scattered bits of paper as it went. Then a piece of the burning paper blew against Nellie's apron and the next instant that was blazing, and Nellie screaming with fright, while the other children ran crying into the inner room--all but Ted. He--petrified with terror--stood still with mouth and eyes wide open, gazing at the fiery stream rolling over the table.

It all happened in two or three seconds, but Nan did not lose her head. She jerked off Nellie's apron without regard to fastenings, and crammed it into the coalhod, then snatching up her old shawl which was lying on the lounge, she threw it over the burning lamp and gathered it closely over lamp, paper and all, so smothering the flames. In two minutes the danger was over, Nan had lighted another lamp that Nellie brought her, and the frightened children came creeping slowly back to the table.

Teddy did not care for paper men or animals any more that night. He was ready to go to bed, and Nellie undressed him and put him there, but the others sat up until the father and mother came home, all eager to tell the story of their danger and of Nan's bravery. The mother's eyes filled with tears as she put her arms about as many of the children as she could gather into them and looked at Nan in silent gratitude, while the father laid his hand kindly on the girl's brown hair as he said, gravely,

"Child, you've earned your place in this home. As long as I'm able to work you're just as welcome here as the rest--you and the baby too."

Nan's eyes were shining happily.

"'Twas nothing much to do," she answered, "and I'll find some way to pay for Little Brother and me if only we can stay here."

Dick had come in soon after his parents, and had listened in gloomy silence to the story of the children.

"Humph!" he said to himself. "Twasn't so awful much to put out that fire. I'd a done it in no time if I'd a been here."

It seemed to Dick that his father and mother were making altogether too much of this strange girl, and the evil spirit of jealousy reared its ugly head in his heart. He wished he had not brought those two home with him, anyhow.

When, the next day, Tode met him on the street and inquired about Nan and Little Brother, Dick replied, gruffly,

"Oh, they're all right 'nough."

"But are they goin' ter stay't your place?" questioned Tode.

"'Spect so." Dick's voice was gruffer than before.

"I'm agoin' 'round there to see 'em to-day," remarked Tode.

Dick made no reply.

Tode repeated, "Don't ye hear? I say I'm agoin' ter see 'em to-day."

"I heard what ye said. S'pose I'm deaf?" and Dick turned his back and marched off.

Tode looked after him angrily. "Like ter punch his head fer him," he said, under his breath. "Would, too, if his folks hadn't let Little Brother stay on there."

Nothing daunted by Dick's unfriendly manner, Tode presented himself that afternoon at Mrs. Hunt's door. He found that good woman and Nan both busy over the paper bags. All the children except Dick were at school, and Little Brother was lying on the old shawl at his sister's feet. Tode gave an awkward nod by way of greeting and dropped down on the floor beside the child.

"Hello, little chap!" he said.

There certainly was a mutual attraction between the two, for the baby again responded to his greeting with a smile, and held out his scrawny little hands.

Tode was delighted. He lifted the child in his arms and sat down with him in an old rocking-chair.

Nan cast a quick, disturbed glance at the two. She had dressed the baby in some clothes that Mrs. Hunt had found for her--a few that had survived Ted's rough usage. They were old but clean, and it was trying to Nan to see Little Brother's pure, sweet face and fresh garments held by Tode's dirty hands against his dirtier jacket. But the baby did not mind. He looked as contented as Tode did, and when the boy's grimy fingers touched his thin cheek, Little Brother laughed a soft, happy, gurgling laugh that was music in Tode's ears. But suddenly the boy's glance took in the contrast between his soiled hand and the little face against which it rested. For a moment he hesitated, then he arose hastily, placed the child gently on the old shawl again and said to Mrs. Hunt,

"Ye ain't got a bit o' soap you could lend me, have ye?"

Mrs. Hunt looked at him inquiringly, then she answered a little unwillingly, for even soap costs money, "You can take that bit on the shelf there."

Tode seized it and vanished. Few things escaped his quick eyes, and he had noticed a sink and a faucet in the hall outside the door. There he rubbed and scrubbed his hands for full five minutes vastly to their improvement, though even then he looked at them doubtfully.

"Can't do no better," he muttered, as he wiped them--well, he had only one place to wipe them, and he did the best he could. When he went back he glanced somewhat sheepishly at Mrs. Hunt as he put the remains of the soap back on the shelf, and again took up the baby. Nan smiled at him but she made no remark, and tried not to look at his jacket.

After he had gone Mrs. Hunt asked, thoughtfully, "How long have you known that boy, Nan?"

"I never saw him until yesterday," answered the girl. "He was good to me then."

"Yes, I know, an' of course you don't want to forget that, but, Nan, I'm afraid he's a bad boy. Dick says he is. He says he lies and steals and swears. I guess you don't want to have much to do with him."

Nan looked troubled. She answered, slowly,

"I guess he hasn't had much of a chance, Mrs. Hunt. He can't remember anything about his father and mother, and he says he's never had any home except the street. Do you s'pose 'twill hurt for him to come here sometimes to see Little Brother? 'Seems as if it might help him to be a better boy. He likes Little Brother."

For a moment Mrs. Hunt was silent. She was thinking how hard she tried to bring up her children to be good boys and girls, and yet they were not always good. She wondered what kind of a boy her Dick would have been if he, like Tode, had had no home and no one to keep him from evil ways.

"If that's so, there's some excuse for him," she said, in response to Nan's plea for Tode.

"P'raps 'twill help him somehow if he gets to carin' for that innocent baby, an' I don't mind his comin' here sometimes, only be careful that you don't learn any evil from him, my dear," and she leaned over and kissed the girl's cheek.

"Oh, Mrs. Hunt, I must be good always, you know, for Little Brother's sake. I can't ever forget or break my promise to mother," Nan answered, earnestly. And Mrs. Hunt, as she saw the solemn look in the dark eyes uplifted to her own, felt that she need not worry about Nan and Tode.

III. AN ACCIDENT

Tode Bryan was sauntering down the street, his hands in his pockets, as usual, when he was not selling papers. He was whistling a lively tune, but he was on the lookout for anything interesting that might happen. As he passed a fruit stand kept by an old woman, he slyly snatched a handful of peanuts which he ate as he went on. He had sold out his papers more quickly than usual, for it was still early in the evening, and the streets were full of business-men on their way to their homes.

Suddenly the boy stopped short and listened, and the next moment there was a general rush into doorways and side streets as a fire-engine came dashing around the corner, while the police rushed from side to side clearing the way through the narrow street.

As the engine passed, Tode, like every other boy within sight or hearing, raced madly after it, shouting and yelling "fire" with all the power of his healthy lungs. Hearing somebody say where the fire was, he slipped through a narrow cross street and an alley, so coming out ahead of the engine which the next moment swung around the nearest corner.

An old man was just crossing the street, and as he heard the clang of the gong and the clatter of the engine, he looked about in a dazed, frightened way, and, instead of hurrying across, hesitated a moment and then turned uncertainly back. The driver did his best to avoid him but when the engine had passed the old man lay motionless upon the ground.

Instantly a crowd gathered about him and Tode pressed forward to the front rank. One policeman was raising the old man's head and another was asking if anybody knew who the injured man was.

It was Tode, who, peering curiously at the pale face, remarked,

"I know him. He buys papers o' me."

"What's his name? Where does he live?" questioned the officer.

"Do' know. He keeps a bookstand down on School street."

26

"Well, we'll have to send him to the hospital. Ring up the ambulance, Dick," said the officer to his companion.

Tode was just dashing off after the engine when one of the policemen collared him.

"Here you!" he exclaimed. "None o' your cuttin' off! If you know this man you've got to go to the hospital an' 'dentify him."

Tode looked uncomfortable and tried to squirm out of the man's grasp--a fruitless effort, for his strength availed nothing against that iron grip. The boy had no idea what "'dentify" might mean but he had his reasons for preferring to keep at a distance from the guardians of the law. There was no help for it, however, so with many inward misgivings, he submitted and waited for the ambulance. When it appeared the still insensible old man was lifted in and Tode was ordered to the front seat where he rode securely between the driver and the policeman. The boy had never before been in a hospital and he felt very ill at ease when he found himself inside the building with its big rooms and long bare halls. He was left alone with the policeman for a while, and then both of them were called into another room and questioned in regard to the accident. Finally Tode was dismissed with strict orders to return the next day.

"He'll be here. I know him, an' if he don't show up, you jest send me word an' I'll find him for ye," the officer said to the doctor, with a threatening glance at the boy.

Tode said nothing, but in his heart he was determined not to return the next day. The officer, however, kept his eye on him, and the next afternoon pounced upon him and put him on a street car with strict orders to the conductor not to let him off until he reached the hospital. So finding himself thus under watch and ward, Tode concluded that he might as well obey orders, and he rang the bell at the hospital door. He was met by the doctor whom he had seen the night before, and taken at once to the ward where the injured man was lying.

As Tode gazed around the long room with its rows of white beds, a feeling of awe stole over him. He wanted to get away, for he did not know what to do or say.

The old man was lying as if asleep, but when the doctor spoke to him he looked up and his dim eyes brightened at sight of the familiar face of the boy.

"Oh, bishop, it's you is it? Got a paper for me?" he said with a feeble smile.

Tode wriggled uneasily as he answered gruffly, "Guess ye don't want none to-day, do ye?"

"No, I don't believe I do. You can bring me one to-morrow, bishop," and as he spoke the old man closed his eyes again, and turned his face away with a weary sigh.

"Come away now," said the doctor, and once outside the door he added, "He hasn't said as much as that before. Seeing some one he knew aroused him as I hoped it would. Why does he call you bishop?"

"I do' know," replied Tode, indifferently.

"Well, you must come again to-morrow. Here's a car ticket and a quarter. I'll give you the same when you come to-morrow. Be here about this time, will you?"

"All right--I'll come," answered the boy to whom the quarter was an inducement.

The old man remained at the hospital for several weeks and Tode continued to visit him there at first for the sake of the money and because he dared not disobey the doctor's orders, but after a while he became rather proud of the old man's evident liking for him, and he would often sit and talk with him for half an hour at a time.

One day Tode inquired curiously, "What d' ye call me bishop for? 'Tain't my name."

And the old man answered dreamily, "You remind me of a boy I knew when I was about your age. He used to say that he was going to be a bishop when he grew up and so we boys always called him 'bishop.'"

"An' did he?" questioned Tode.

"Become a bishop? No, he entered the army and died in his first battle."

"W'at's a bishop, anyhow?" asked Tode, after a moment's silence.

"You know what a minister is, Tode?"

"A preacher, ye mean?"

"Yes, a minister is a preacher. A bishop is a sort of head preacher--ranking higher, you know."

Tode nodded. "I'd rather be a soldier like that feller you knew," he remarked.

A day came when the old man was pronounced well enough to leave the hospital and the doctor ordered Tode to be on hand to take him home. The boy did not object. He was rather curious to see the little place in the rear of the bookstand where the old man lived alone. Since the accident the stand had been closed and Tode helped to open and air the room and then made a fire in the stove. When this was done the old man gave him money to buy materials for supper which of course the boy shared.

After this he came daily to the place to run errands or do anything that was wanted, and by degrees the old man came to depend more and more upon him until the business of the little stand fell almost wholly into the boy's hands, for the owner's head still troubled him and he could not think clearly. It was a great relief to him to have some one to look after everything for him. Tode liked it and the business prospered in his hands. If he lacked experience, he was quicker and sharper than the old man. The two took their meals together, and at night Tode slept on a blanket on the floor, and was more comfortable and prosperous than he had ever been in his life before. He had money to spend too, for old Mr. Carey never asked for any account of the sums that passed through the boy's hands. So he himself was undisturbed by troublesome questions and figures, the old man was content now, and each day found him a little weaker and feebler. Tode noticed this but he gave no thought to the matter. Why borrow trouble when things were so much to his mind? Tode lived in the present.

He still sold the evening papers, considering it wise to keep possession of his route against future need, and never a week passed that he did not see Little Brother at least twice. He would have liked to see the child every day, but he knew instinctively that he was not a favorite with the Hunts, and that knowledge made him ill at ease with them. But it could not keep him away altogether. He found too much satisfaction in Little Brother's love for him.

More than once Mrs. Hunt had remarked to Nan that she didn't "see what in the world made the baby so fond of that rough, dirty boy." Nan herself wondered at it though she kept always a grateful remembrance of Tode's kindness when she first met him.

Tode often brought little gifts to the child, and would have given him much more, but Nan would not allow it. The two had a long argument over the matter one day. It was a bright, sunny morning and Mrs. Hunt had said that the baby ought to be out in the fresh air, so Nan had taken him to the Common, and sat there keeping ever a watchful eye for their enemy, Mary Leary. Tode going down Beacon street espied the two and forgetting all about the errand on which he was bound, promptly joined them.

"He's gettin' fat--he is," the boy remarked, poking his finger at the dimple in the baby's cheek, then drawing it quickly away again with an uncomfortable expression. Tode never cared how dirty his hands were except when he saw them in contrast with Little Brother's pure face.

"Yes, he's getting well and strong," assented Nan, with a happy smile.

"I say, Nan, w'at's the reason you won't let me pay for his milk?" asked Tode, after a little.

Then it was Nan's turn to look uncomfortable, and the color rose in her cheeks as she answered, "I can pay now for all he needs. You know Mrs. Hunt gets a double quantity of bags and I work on them every day."

But this answer did not satisfy Tode. "That don't make no diff'runce," he growled. "Don't see why you won't let me do nothin' for him," and he cast a gloomy glance at the baby, but Little Brother laughed up at him and the gloom speedily melted away. After a moment's silence he added, slowly, "It's comin' cold weather. He'll want a jacket or somethin', won't he?"

"He'll have to have some warm clothes," replied Nan, thoughtfully, "but I can get them--I guess."

Tode turned upon her fiercely. "I s'pose you'd let him freeze to death 'fore you'd let me buy him any clothes," he burst out, angrily. "I sh'd like ter know w'at's the matter with ye, anyhow. Has that measly Dick Hunt ben stuffin' ye 'bout me?"

Nan coloured again and dropped her eyes.

"Say--has he? I'll give it ter him next time I catch him out!" and Tode ground his heel suggestively into the gravel walk.

"Oh, Tode, don't! Please don't fight Dick," pleaded Nan. "How can you when his mother's so good to Little Brother?"

"Don't care 'f she is. He ain't," was Tode's surly reply. "He don't want you'n him to stay there."

Nan's eyes were full of uneasiness.

"Did he say so?" she questioned, for she had noticed Dick's coldness and been vaguely disturbed by it.

The boy nodded. "Yes," he said, "he tol' me so. Said there's 'nough fer his father ter feed 'thout you'n him," and he pointed to the baby.

31

"But I work," pleaded Nan. "I pay for all we eat."

"But ye don't pay fer the rent an' the fire, an'--an' everything," Tode replied, with a note of triumph in his voice, "so now, ye better let me pay fer Little Brother an' then you c'n pay the rest."

Nan hesitated and her face was troubled. Finally she lifted her dark eyes to his and said bravely, "Tode, I guess I ought to tell you just why I couldn't anyway let you do for Little Brother as you want to. It's because--because you don't get your money the right way."

"Who says I don't? Did that Dick Hunt say so? I'll"--began Tode, fiercely, but Nan laid her hand on his arm and looked steadily into his face.

"Tode," she said, earnestly, "if you will look straight into Little Brother's eyes and tell me that you never steal--I'll believe you."

"I never"--began the boy, boldly; then he met a grave, sweet glance from the baby's big blue eyes, and he hesitated. The lying words died on his tongue, and turning his eyes away from the little face that he loved, he said gloomily, "What's that got to do with it anyhow? S'posin' I do hook a han'ful of peanuts sometimes. That ain't nothin'."

"Tode, do you want Little Brother to hook a handful of peanuts sometimes when he gets big?" asked Nan, quietly.

The boy turned his eyes again to the baby face and the hot blood burned in his own as he answered, quickly, "'Course I don't. He won't be that sort."

"No, he won't, if I can help it," replied Nan, gravely.

Tode dug his toe into the dirt in silence. Nan added, "Tode, by and by, when he gets bigger, would you want him to know that you were a thief?"

When Tode looked up there was a strange gravity in his eyes, and his lips were set in an expression of stern resolve.

"I've got ter quit it," he said, solemnly, "an' I will. Say, Nan," he added, wistfully, "if I quit now, ye wont ever let him know I used ter be--what you said, will ye?"

"No, Tode, never," answered Nan, quickly and earnestly. "And Tode, if you'll stick to it, and not steal or lie or swear, I shan't mind your helping me get things for Little Brother."

The boy's face brightened, and he drew himself up proudly. "It's a bargain, then," he said.

Nan looked at him thoughtfully. "I don't believe you know how hard it will be, Tode. I find it's awful hard to break myself of bad habits, and I don't s'pose you've ever tried to before, have you?"

Tode considered the question. "Guess not," he said, slowly, after a pause.

"Then I'm afraid you'll find you can't stop doing those bad things all at once. But you'll keep on trying, Tode. You won't give up 'cause it's hard work," Nan pleaded, anxiously.

"Nope," answered the boy, briefly, with a glance at the soft little fingers that were clasped about one of his.

When Nan went home he went with her to the door, loth to lose sight of the only creature in the world for whom he cared. As the door closed behind the two, he walked on thinking over what Nan had said. Much of it seemed to him "girls' stuff an' nonsense." "As if a fella couldn't stop swipin' things if he wanted to!" he said to himself.

As he went on he passed a fruit stand where a man was buying some bananas. In putting his change into his pocket he dropped a nickel, which rolled toward Tode who promptly set his foot on it, and then pretending to pull a rag off his torn trousers, he picked up the coin and went on chuckling over his "luck." But suddenly he stopped short and the hot color rose in his cheeks as he exclaimed with an oath,

"Done it again!"

He looked around for the man, but he had disappeared, and with an angry grunt Tode flung the nickel into the gutter and went on, beginning so soon to realise that evil habits are not overcome by simply resolving to conquer them. Tode never had made any such attempt before, and the discovery had rather a depressing effect on him. It made him cross, too, but to his credit be it said, the thought of giving up the struggle never once occurred to him.

He found old Mr. Carey asleep in his chair, and he awoke him roughly.

"See here!" he exclaimed, sharply. "Is this the way you 'tend to business when I'm gone? Some cove might a stole every book an' paper on the stand, and cleaned out the cash, too." He pulled open the drawer as he spoke. "No thanks to you that 'tain't empty," he grumbled. He had never spoken so sharply before, and the old man was vaguely disturbed by it. He got up and walked feebly across the room, rubbing his trembling fingers through his grey hair in a troubled fashion, as he answered slowly,

"Yes, yes, bishop--you're right. It was very careless of me to go to sleep so. I don't see how I came to do it. I'm afraid I'm breaking down, my boy--breaking down," he added, sadly.

As Tode looked at the old man's dim eyes and shaking hands a feeling of sympathy and compassion stole into his heart, and his voice softened as he said, "Oh, well, it's all right this time. Reckon I'll have to run the business altogether till you get better."

"I'm afraid you will, bishop. I'm not much good anyhow, nowadays," and the old man dropped again into his chair with a heavy sigh.

The weeks that followed were the most miserable weeks of Tode Byran's short life. He found out some things about himself that he had never before suspected. It was wholesome knowledge, but it was not pleasant to find that in spite of his strongest resolutions, those nimble fingers of his would pick up nuts and apples from street stands and his quick tongue would rattle off lies and evil words before he could remember to stop it. The other boys found him a most unpleasant companion in these days, for his continual failures made him cross and moody. He would speedily have given up the struggle but for Little Brother. Several times he did give it up

34

for a week or two, but then he staid away from the Hunts' rooms until he grew so hungry for a sight of the baby face that he could stay away no longer. Nan came to understand what these absences meant, and always when he reappeared she would speak a word of encouragement and faith in his final victory. Tode had not cared at all for Nan at first, but in these days of struggle and failure he began to value her steadfast faith in him, and again and again he renewed his vow to make himself "fit to help bring up Little Brother," as he expressed it.

It was one day toward the close of winter that Tode noticed that Mr. Carey seemed more than usually dull and listless, dropping into a doze even while the boy was speaking to him, and he went to bed directly after supper. When the boy awoke the next morning the old man lay just as he had fallen asleep. He did not answer when Tode spoke to him, and his hands were cold as ice to the boy's touch.

Tode did not know what to do, but he finally hunted up the policeman, who knew him, and the two went back together and found the old man dead. As no relatives appeared, the city authorities took charge of the funeral, the books and the few pieces of furniture were sold to pay the expenses, and Tode found himself once more a homeless waif. He had not minded it before, but his brief experience of even this poor home had unfitted him for living and sleeping in the streets. He found it unpleasant too, to have no money except the little he could earn selling papers. He set himself to face his future in earnest, and came to the conclusion that it was time for him to get into some better paying business. After thinking over the matter for several days he went to Nan.

"You know them doughnuts you made th' other day?" he began.

"Yes," replied Nan, wonderingly. Mrs. Hunt had taught her to make various simple dishes, and as Tode had happened in the day she made her first doughnuts, she had given him a couple, which he had pronounced "prime!"

Now he went on, "I don't want to sleep 'round the streets any more. I'm sick of it, but I can't make money 'nough off papers to do anything else. I'm thinkin' of settin' up a stand."

"A bookstand, Tode?" questioned Nan, interestedly.

"No--a eatin' stand--fer the fellers ye know--newsboys an' such. 'F you'll make doughnuts an' gingerbread an' san'wiches fer me, I bet all the fellers'll come fer 'em."

"Now that ain't a bad idea, Tode," said Mrs. Hunt, looking up from her work. "Of course the boys would buy good homemade food instead of the trash they get from the cheap eatin' houses, an' Nan, I shouldn't wonder if you could earn more that way than by workin' at these bags."

Nan considered the matter thoughtfully, and finally agreed to give it a trial, and Tode went off highly pleased.

It took him two weeks to save enough to start his stand even in the simplest fashion, but when he did open it, he at first did a flourishing business. In the beginning the boys patronised him partly from curiosity and partly from good fellowship, but Nan's cookery found favour with them at once, and "Tode's Corner" soon became the favorite lunch counter for the city newsboys, and Tode's pockets were better filled than they had been since Mr. Carey's death.

For several weeks all went well, and the boy began to consider himself on the high road to fortune, but then came a setback.

One day his stand was surrounded by a crowd of boys all clamoring to be served at once, when the big fellow who had taken possession of Tode's newspaper route, months before, came along. He had never forgotten or forgiven the boy for getting the better of him on that occasion, and now he thought he saw a chance for revenge.

Creeping up behind the group of hungry boys, he suddenly hit one of them a stinging blow on the face, and as this one turned and struck back angrily at him, the big fellow flung him back with all his strength against Tode's stand. The stand was an old one and rickety--Tode had bought it secondhand--and it went down with a crash, carrying cookies, doughnuts, gingerbread, coffee, sandwiches, cups, plates and boys in one promiscuous mixture. Before the boys could struggle to their feet, Carrots, with his hands full of gingerbread, had disappeared around the nearest corner. There was a wild rush and a scramble, and when two minutes later, Tode stood gazing mournfully at the wreck, not an eatable bit remained. The boys had considered the wreckage as their lawful spoils, and every one of them had snatched as much as he could.

Later, however, their sense of justice led some of them to express, after their rough fashion, sympathy for Tode, and disapproval of his enemy's revengeful act. Besides, a few of them had enough conscience to acknowledge to themselves that they had not been entirely blameless. The result was that half a dozen of them went to Tode the next day and offered to "chip in" and set him up again.

Tode appreciated the spirit that prompted the offer, but he was also shrewd enough to foresee that should he accept it, these boys would expect favours in the way of prices and quantities when they dealt with him in the future, and so he declined.

"Reckin I can stan' on my own feet, boys," he answered. "I've been a-tinkerin' up the ol' stand, an' I'm a-goin' to start in again to-morrow. You fellers come here an' get yer breakfast, an' that's all the help I'll ask, 'cept that ev'ry last one o' ye'll give that Carrots a kick fer me."

"We will that!" shouted the boys. "We'll make him sorry fer himself!"

And the next day their sympathy took the practical form that Tode had suggested, for every one of them that had any money to spend, spent it at "Tode's Corner," so that his stand was cleared again, but in a very satisfactory fashion--a fashion that filled his pockets with dimes and nickels.

IV. TODE MEETS THE BISHOP

Sundays were Tode's dreariest days. He found that it did not pay to keep his stand open later than ten o'clock, and then after he had spent an hour with Little Brother and Nan, the time hung heavy on his hands. Sometimes he pored over a newspaper for a while, sometimes over something even more objectionable than the Sunday newspaper, and for the rest, he loafed around street corners and wharves with other homeless boys like himself.

One Sunday morning he was listlessly reading over some play-bills pasted on a fence, when the word "bishop" caught his eye, and he spelled out the announcement that a well-known bishop was to speak in St. Mark's Church, that afternoon.

"Cracky! I'd like to see a live bishop. B'lieve I'll go," he said to himself. Then looking down at his ragged trousers and dirty jacket, he added with a grin, "'Spect some o' them nobs'll most have a fit to see me there."

Nevertheless he determined to go. Old Mr. Carey had never called him anything but "bishop," and now the boy had a queer feeling as he read that word on the bill--a feeling that this bishop whom he had never seen had yet in some way something to do with him--though in what way he could not imagine.

He thought over the matter through the hours that followed, sometimes deciding that he would go, and again that he wouldn't, but he found out where St. Mark's Church was, and at three o'clock he was there.

He gave a little start and a shadow fell upon his face as he saw the pillared porch and the stone stairway. He seemed to see himself running up those stairs and stuffing that stolen pocketbook into the pastor's box that he remembered so clearly. These thoughts were not pleasant ones to him now, and Tode stopped hesitatingly, undecided whether to go on or to go in. It was early yet and no one was entering though the doors stood invitingly open.

While he hesitated, the sexton came out to the steps. Tode remembered him too, and looked at him with a grin that exasperated the man. "Get out o' this!" he exclaimed, roughly. "We don't want any o' your sort 'round here."

Of course that settled the matter for Tode. He was determined to go in now anyhow, but he knew better than to attempt it just then.

"Who wants to go int' yer ol' church," he muttered as he turned away. The man growled a surly response but Tode did not look back.

On the corner he stopped, wondering how he could best elude the unfriendly sexton and slip into the building, without his knowledge. He dropped down on the curbstone and sat there thinking for some time. At last a voice above him said quietly,

"Well, my boy, aren't you coming to church?"

Tode looked up, up a long way it seemed to him, into such a face as he had never before looked into. Instinctively he arose and stepped back that he might see more plainly those clear blue eyes and that strong, tender mouth. The boy gazed and gazed, forgetting utterly to answer.

"You are coming into church with me, aren't you?"

So the question was repeated, and Tode, still lookingly earnestly up into the man's face, nodded silently.

"That's right, my son--come," and a large, kindly hand was laid gently upon the boy's shoulder.

Without a word he walked on beside the stranger.

The sexton was standing in the vestibule as the two approached. A look of blank amazement swept across his face at sight of the boy in such company. He said no word, however, only stepped aside with a bow, but his eyes followed the two as they passed into the church together, and he muttered a few angry words under his breath.

As for Tode, some strange influence seemed to have taken possession of him, for he forgot to exult over the surly sexton. He passed him without a thought indeed, feeling nothing but a strange, happy wonder at the companionship in which he found himself.

The stranger led him up the aisle to one of the best pews, and motioned him in. Silently the boy obeyed. Then the man looking down with his rare, beautiful smile into the uplifted face, gently raised Tode's ragged cap from his rough hair, and laid it on the cushioned seat beside him. Then he went away, and Tode felt as if the sunlight had been suddenly darkened. His eyes followed the tall, strong figure longingly until it disappeared--then he looked about him, at the beautiful interior of the church. The boy had never been in such a place before, and he gazed wonderingly at the frescoes, the rich colours in the windows, the dark carved woodwork and the wide chancel and pulpit.

"Wat's it all for, I wonder," he said, half aloud, and then started and flushed as his own voice broke the beautiful, solemn silence.

People were beginning to come in and filling the seats about him, and many curious and astonished glances fell upon the boy, but he did not notice them. Presently a soft, low strain of music stole out upon the stillness. Surely a master hand touched the keys that day, for the street boy sat like a statue listening eagerly to the sweet sounds, and suddenly he found his cheeks wet. He dashed his hand impatiently across them wondering what was the matter with him, for tears were strangers to Tode's eyes, but in spite of himself they filled again, till he almost wished the music would cease--almost but not quite, for that strange happiness thrilled his heart as he listened.

Then far-off voices began to sing, coming nerrer and nearer, until a long line of white-robed men and boys appeared, singing as they walked, and last of all came the kingly stranger who had brought Tode into the church, and he went to the lectern and began to read.

"The--bishop!" Tode breathed the words softly, in a mixture of wonder and delight, as he suddenly realised who this man must be.

He sat through the remainder of the service in a dreamy state of strange enjoyment. He did not understand why the people around him stood or knelt at intervals. He did not care. When the bishop prayed, Tode looked around, wondering whom he was calling "Lord." He concluded that it must be the one who made the music.

He listened eagerly, breathlessly, to the sermon, understanding almost nothing of what was said, but simply drinking in the words spoken by that rich, sweet voice, that touched something within him, something that only Little Brother had ever touched before. Yet this was different from the feeling that the baby had awakened in the boy's heart. He loved the baby dearly, but to this great, grand man, who stood there above him wearing the strange dress that he had never before seen a man wear--to him the boy's whole heart seemed to go out in reverent admiration and desire. He knew that he would do anything that this man might ask of him. He could refuse him nothing.

"Ye are not your own. Ye are bought with a price."

These words, repeated again and again, fixed themselves in Tode's memory with no effort of his own. Buying and selling were matters quite in his line now, but he did not understand this. He puzzled over it awhile, then put it aside to be thought out at another time.

When the service was over, Tode watched the long line of choir boys pass slowly out, and his eyes followed the tall figure of the bishop till it disappeared from his wistful gaze. Then he looked about upon the kneeling congregation, wondering if the people were going to stay there all day. The bishop was gone, the music had ceased, and Tode did not want to stay any longer. He slipped silently out of the pew and left the church.

That evening he wandered off by himself, avoiding the Sunday gathering-places of the boys, and thinking over the new experiences of the afternoon. The words the bishop had repeated so often sung themselves over and over in his ears.

"Ye are not your own. Ye are bought with a price."

"Don't mean me, anyhow," he thought, "'cause I b'long ter myself, sure 'nough. Nobody ever bought me 't ever I heard of. Wonder who that Jesus is, he talked about so much. I wish--I wish he'd talk ter me--that bishop."

All the strange happiness that had filled his heart during the service in the church, was gone now. He did not feel happy at all. On the contrary, he felt wretched and utterly miserable. He had begun to have a distinct pride and satisfaction in himself lately, since he had stopped lying and stealing, and had set up in business for himself, and especially since Mrs. Hunt had begun to look upon him with more favour, as he knew she had--but somehow now all this seemed worthless. Although he had not understood the bishop's sermon, it seemed to have unsettled Tode's mind, and awakened a vague miserable dissatisfaction with himself. He was not used to such feelings. He didn't like them, and he grew cross and ugly when he found himself unable to shake them off.

He had wandered to the quiet corner of the wharf, where he and Nan and Little Brother had spent the first hours of their acquaintance, and he stood leaning against that same post, looking gloomily down into the water, when a lean, rough dog crept slowly toward him, wagging his stumpy tail and looking into the boy's face with eyes that pleaded for a friendly word. Generally Tode would have responded to the mute appeal, but now he felt so miserable himself, that he longed to make somebody or something else miserable too, so instead of a pat, he gave the dog a kick that sent it limping off with a yelp of pain and remonstrance. He had made another creature as miserable as himself, but somehow it didn't seem to lessen his own wretchedness. Indeed, he couldn't help feeling that he had done a mean, cowardly thing, and Tode never liked to feel himself a coward. He looked after the dog. It had crawled into a corner and was licking the injured paw. Tode walked toward the poor creature that looked at him suspiciously, yet with a faint little wag of its tail, as showing its readiness to forgive and forget, while at the same time ready to run if more abuse threatened.

Tode stooped and called, "Come here, sir!" and, after a moment's hesitation, the dog crept slowly toward him with a low whine, still keeping his bright eyes fastened on the boy's.

"Poor old fellow," Tode said, gently, patting the dog's rough head. "Is it hurt? Let me see." He felt of the leg, the dog standing quietly beside him.

"'Tain't broken. It'll be all right pretty soon. What's your name?" Tode said, and the dog rubbed his head against the boy's knee and tried to say with his eloquent eyes what his dumb lips could not utter.

"Got none--ye mean? You're a street dog--like me," the boy added. "Well, guess I'll go home an' get some supper," and he walked slowly away and presently forgot all about the dog.

He had lately hired a tiny garret room where he slept, and kept his supplies when his stand was closed. He went there now and ate his lonely supper. It had never before seemed lonely to him, but somehow to-night it did. He hurried down the food and started to go out again. As he opened his door, he heard a faint sound, and something moved on the dark landing.

"Who's there?" he called, sharply.

A low whine answered him, and from out the gloom two eyes gleamed and glittered. Tode peered into the shadow, then he laughed.

"So it's you, is it? You must have tagged me home. Come in here then if you want to," and he flung his door wide open and stepped back into the room.

Then out of the shadows of the dark landing the dog came slowly and warily, ready to turn and slink off if he met no welcome, but Tode was in the mood when even a strange dog was better than his own company. He fed the half-starved creature with some stale sandwiches, and then talked to him and tried to teach him some tricks until to his own surprise he heard the city clocks striking nine, and the long, lonely evening he had dreaded was gone.

"Well now, you're a heap o' company," he said to the dog. "I've a good mind ter keep ye. Say, d'ye wan' ter stay, ol' feller?"

The dog wagged his abbreviated tail, licked Tode's fingers, and rubbed his head against the ragged trousers of his new friend.

"Ye do, hey! Well, I'll keep ye ter-night, anyhow. Le' see, what'll I call ye? You've got ter have a name. S'posin' I call ye Tag. That do--hey, Tag?"

The dog gave a quick, short bark and limped gaily about the boy's feet.

"All right--we'll call ye Tag then. Now then, there's yer bed," and he threw into a corner an old piece of carpet that he had picked up on a vacant lot. The dog understood and settled himself with a long, contented sigh, as if he would have said:

"At last I've found a master and a home."

In a day or two Tag's lameness disappeared, and his devotion to his new master was unbounded. Tode found him useful, too, for he kept vigilant watch when the boy was busy at his stand, and suffered no thievish fingers to snatch anything when Tode's eyes and fingers were too busy for him to be on the lookout. The dog was such a loving, intelligent little creature, that he quickly won his way into Nan's heart, and he evidently considered himself the guardian of Little Brother from the first day that he saw Tode and the child together. Some dogs have a way of reading hearts, and Tag knew within two minutes that Tode loved every lock on Little Brother's sunny head.

A few days after that Sabbath that the boy was never to forget, he went to see Nan and the baby, and in the course of his visit, remarked,

"Nan, I seen the bishop last Sunday."

"What bishop?" inquired Nan.

"The one that talked at the big, stone church--St. Mark's, they call it."

"I wonder 't they let you in, if you wore them ragged duds," remarked Mrs. Hunt.

"The bishop asked me to go in an' he took me in himself," retorted Tode, defiantly.

"For the land's sake," exclaimed Mrs. Hunt. "He must be a queer kind of a bishop!"

"A splendid kind of a bishop, I should think," put in Nan, and the boy responded quickly,

"He is so! I never see a man like him."

"Never see a man like him? What d'ye mean, Tode?" questioned Mrs. Hunt.

Tode looked at her as he answered slowly, "He's a great big man--looks like a king--an' his eyes look right through a feller, but they don't hurt. They ain't sharp. They're soft, an'--an'--I guess they look like a mother's eyes would. I d'know much 'bout mothers, 'cause I never had one, but I should think they'd look like his do. I tell ye," Tode faced Mrs. Hunt and spoke earnestly, "a feller'd do 'most anything that that bishop asked him to-- couldn't help it."

Mrs. Hunt stared in amazement at the boy. His eyes were glowing and in his voice there was a ring of deep feeling that she had never before heard in it. It made her vaguely uncomfortable. Her Dick had never spoken so about any bishop, nor indeed, about anybody else, and here was this rough street boy whom she considered quite unfit to associate with Dick--and the bishop himself had taken him into church.

Mrs. Hunt spoke somewhat sharply. "Well, I must say you were a queer-lookin' one to set in a pew in a church like St. Mark's."

Nan looked distressed, and Tode glanced uneasily at his garments. They certainly were about as bad as they could be. Even pins and twine could not hold them together much longer.

45

"Tode," Mrs. Hunt went on, "I think it's high time you got yourself some better clothes. Dear knows, you need 'em if ever a boy did, an' certainly you must have money 'nough now."

"'Spect I have. I never thought about it," replied Tode.

"Well, you'd better think about it, an' 'tend to it right away. 'F you're goin' to church with bishops you'd ought to look respectable, anyhow."

Something in the tone and emphasis with which Mrs. Hunt spoke brought the colour into Tode's brown cheeks, while Nan looked at the good woman in surprise and dismay. She did not know how troubled was the mother's heart over her own boy lately, as she saw him growing rough and careless, and that it seemed to her hard that this waif of the streets should be going up while her Dick went down.

Tode thought over what had been said, and the result was that the next time he appeared he was so changed that the good woman looked twice before she recognised him. His clothes had been purchased at a secondhand store, and they might have fitted better than they did, but they were a vast improvement on what he had worn before. He had scrubbed his face as well as his hands this time, and had combed his rough hair as well as he could with the broken bit of comb which was all he possessed in the way of toilet appliances. It is no easy matter for a boy to keep himself well washed and brushed with no face cloth or towel or brush, and no wash basin save the public sink. Tode had done his best however, and Nan looked at him in pleased surprise.

"You do look nice, Tode," she said, and the boy's face brightened with satisfaction.

All through that week Tode told himself that he would not go to the church again, yet day by day the longing grew to see the bishop's face once more and to hear his voice.

"W'at's the use! O'ny makes a feller feel meaner 'n dirt," he said to himself again and again, yet the next Sabbath afternoon found him hanging about

St. Mark's hoping that the bishop would ask him in again. But the minutes passed and the bishop did not appear.

"Maybe he's gone in aready," the boy thought, peering cautiously through the pillars of the entrance. There was no one in sight, and Tode crept quietly across the porch through the wide vestibule to the church door. Only the sexton was there, and his back was toward the boy as he stood looking out of the opposite door.

"Now's my time," thought Tode, and he ran swiftly and silently up the aisle to the pew where the bishop had placed him. There he hesitated. He was not sure which of several pews was the one, but with a quick glance at the sexton's back, he slipped into the nearest, and hearing the man's footsteps approaching, dropped to the floor and crawled under the seat.

The sexton came slowly down the aisle, stopping here and there to arrange books or brush off a dusty spot. He even entered the pew where Tode was, and moved the books in the rack in front, but the boy lay motionless in the shadow, and the man passed on without discovering him.

Then the people began to come in, and Tode was just about to get up and sit on the seat, when a lady and a little girl entered the pew.

The boy groaned inwardly. "They'll screech if I get up now," he thought. "Nothin' for it but to lay here till it's over. Wal', I c'n hear him anyhow."

"Him," in Tode's thought was the bishop, and he waited patiently through the early part of the service, longing to hear again that rich, strong, thrilling voice. But alas for Tode! It was not the bishop who preached that day. It was a stranger, whose low monotonous voice reached the boy so indistinctly, that he soon gave up all attempts to listen, and before the sermon was half over he was sound asleep. Fortunately he was used to hard resting-places, and he slept so quietly that the occupants of the pew did not discover his presence at all.

The music of the choir and of the organ mingled with the boy's dreams, but did not arouse him, and when the people departed and the sexton closed the church and went home, Tode still slept on in darkness and solitude.

Usually there was an evening service, but on this occasion it was omitted, the rector being ill, so when Tode at last opened his eyes, it was to find all dark and silent about him. As he started up his head struck the bottom of the seat with a force that made him cry out and drop back again. Then as he lay there he put out his hands, and feeling the cushioned seat over his head, he knew where he was and guessed what had happened.

"Wal! I was a chump to go to sleep here!" he muttered, slowly, rising with hands outstretched. "'Spect I'll have ter get out of the window."

The street lights shining through the stained glass made a faint twilight in the church, but there was something weird and strange about being there alone at that hour that set the boy's heart to beating faster than usual.

He went to one of the windows and felt about for the fastenings, but he could not reach them. They were too high. He tried them all, but none were within his reach. Then he sat down in one of the pews and wondered what he should do next. He was wide awake now. It seemed to him that he could not close his eyes again that night, and indeed it was long after midnight before he did. He felt strangely lonely as he sat there through those endless hours, dimly hearing the voices and footsteps in the street without grow fewer and fainter, till all was silent save the clocks that rang out the creeping hours to his weary ears. At last his tired eyes closed and he slipped down on the cushioned seat and slept for a few hours, but he awoke again before daylight.

It was broad daylight outside before it was light enough in the church for the boy to see clearly, and then he looked hopelessly at the high window fastenings. He had tried every door but all were securely locked.

"Nothin' t' do but wait till that ol' cove comes back," he said to himself.

Then a thought flashed across his mind--a thought that made his heart stand still with dread. "S'posin' he don't come till next Sunday?"

Tode knew nothing about midweek or daily services. But he put this terrible thought away from him.

"I'll get out somehow if I have ter smash some o' them pictures," he said aloud, as he looked up at the beautiful windows.

The minutes seemed endless while the boy walked restlessly up and down the aisles thinking of his stand, and of the customers who would seek breakfast there in vain that morning. At last he heard approaching footsteps, then a key rattled in the lock, and Tode instinctively rolled under the nearest pew and lay still, listening to the heavy footsteps of the sexton as he passed slowly about opening doors and windows. The boy waited with what patience he could until the man passed on to the further side of the church, then he slid and crawled along the carpeted aisle until he reached the door, when springing to his feet he made a dash for the street. He heard the sexton shouting angrily after him, but he paid no heed. On and on he ran until he reached his room where Tag gave him a wildly delighted welcome, and in a very short time thereafter the stand at "Tode's Corner" was doing a brisk business.

V. IN THE BISHOP'S HOUSE

Tode's patrons were mostly newsboys of his acquaintance, who came pretty regularly to his stand for breakfast, and generally for a midday meal, lunch or dinner as it might be. Where they took their supper he did not know, but he usually closed his place of business after one o'clock, and spent a couple of hours roaming about the streets doing any odd job that came in his way, if he happened to feel like it, or to be in need of money.

After his meeting with the bishop he often wandered up into the neighbourhood of St. Mark's with a vague hope that he might see again the man who seemed to his boyish imagination a very king among men. It had long been Tode's secret ambition to grow into a big, strong man himself-- bigger and stronger than the common run of men. Now, whenever he thought about it, he said to himself, "Just like the bishop."

But he never met the bishop, and having found out that he did not preach regularly at St. Mark's, Tode never went there after the second time.

One afternoon in late September, the boy was lounging along with Tag at his heels in the neighbourhood of the church, when he heard a great rattling of wheels and clattering of hoofs, and around the corner came a pair of horses dragging a carriage that swung wildly from side to side, as the horses came tearing down the street. There was no one in the carriage, but the driver was puffing along a little way behind, yelling frantically, "Stop 'em! Stop 'em! Why don't ye stop the brutes!"

There were not many people on the street, and the few men within sight seemed not at all anxious to risk life or limb in an attempt to stop horses going at such a reckless pace.

Now Tode was only a little fellow not yet fourteen, but he was strong and lithe as a young Indian, and as to fear--he did not know what it was. As he saw the horses dashing toward him he leaped into the middle of the street and stood there, eyes alert and limbs ready, directly in their pathway. They swerved aside as they approached him, but with a quick upward spring he grabbed the bit of the one nearest him, and hung there with all his weight. This frightened and maddened the horse, and he plunged and reared and flung his head from side to side, until he succeeded in throwing the boy off. The delay however, slight as it was, had given the driver time to come up, and he speedily regained control of his team while a crowd quickly gathered.

Tode had been flung off sidewise, his head striking the curbstone, and there he lay motionless, while faithful Tag crouched beside him, now and then licking the boy's fingers, and whining pitifully as he looked from face to face, as if he would have said,

"Won't some of you help him? I can't."

The crowd pressed about the unconscious boy with a sort of morbid curiosity, one proposing one thing and one another until a policeman came along and promptly sent a summons for an ambulance; but before it appeared, a tall grey-haired man came up the street and stopped to see what was the matter. He was so tall that he could look over the heads of most of the men, and as he saw the white face of the boy lying there in the street, he hastily pushed aside the onlookers as if they had been men of straw, and stooping, lifted the boy in his strong arms.

"Stand back," he cried, his voice ringing out like a trumpet, "would you let the child die in the street?"

They fell back before him, a whisper passing from lip to lip. "It's the bishop!" they said, and some ran before him to open the gate and some to ring the bell of the great house before which the accident had occurred.

Mechanically the bishop thanked them, but he looked at none of them. His eyes were fixed upon the face that lay against his shoulder, the blood dripping slowly from a cut on one side of the head.

The servant who opened the door stared for an instant wonderingly, at his master with the child in his arms, and at the throng pressing curiously after them, but the next moment he recovered from his amazement and, admitting the bishop, politely but firmly shut out the eager throng that would have entered with him. A lank, rough-haired dog attempted to slink in at the bishop's heels, but the servant gave him a kick that made him draw back with a yelp of pain, and he took refuge under the steps where he remained all night, restless and miserable, his quick ears yet ever on the alert for a voice or a step that he knew.

As the door closed behind the bishop, he exclaimed,

"Call Mrs. Martin, Brown, and then send for the doctor. This boy was hurt at our very door."

Brown promptly obeyed both orders, and Mrs. Martin, the housekeeper, hastily prepared a room for the unexpected guest. The doctor soon responded to the summons, but all his efforts failed to restore the boy to consciousness that day. The bishop watched the child as anxiously as if it had been one of his own flesh and blood. He had neither wife nor child, but perhaps all the more for that, his great heart held love enough and to spare for every child that came in his way.

It was near the close of the following day when Tode's eyes slowly opened and he came back to consciousness, but his eyes wandered about the strange room and he still lay silent and motionless. The doctor and the bishop were both beside him at the moment and he glanced from one face to the other in a vague, doubtful fashion. He asked no question, however, and soon his eyes again closed wearily, but this time in sleep, healthful and refreshing, instead of the stupor that had preceded it, and the doctor turned away with an expression of satisfaction.

"He'll pull through now," he said in a low tone. "He's young and full of vitality--he'll soon be all right."

The bishop rubbed his hands with satisfaction. "That's well! That's well!" he exclaimed, heartily.

The doctor looked at him curiously. "Did you ever see the lad before you picked him up yesterday?" he asked.

"No, never," answered the bishop, who naturally had not recognised in Tode the boy whom he had taken into church that Sunday, weeks before.

The doctor shook his head as he drove off and muttered to himself,

"Whoever saw such a man! Who but our bishop would ever think of taking a little street urchin like that right into his home and treating him as if he were his own flesh and blood! Well, well, he himself gets taken in often no doubt in another fashion, but all the same the world would be the better if there were more like him!"

And if the doctor's pronouns were a little mixed he himself understood what he meant, and nobody else had anything to do with the matter.

The next morning Tode awoke again and this time to a full and lively consciousness of his surroundings. It was still early and the nurse was dozing in an easy-chair beside the bed. The boy looked at her curiously, then he raised himself on his elbow and gazed about him, but as he did so he became conscious of a dull throbbing pain in one side of his head and a sick faintness swept over him. It was his first experience of weakness, and it startled him into a faint groan as his head fell back on the pillow.

The sound awoke the nurse, who held a spoonful of medicine to his lips, saying,

"Lie still. The doctor says you must not talk at all until he comes."

"So," thought the boy. "I've got a doctor. Wonder where I am an' what ails me, anyhow."

But that strange weakness made it easy to obey orders and lie still while the nurse bathed his face and hands and freshened up the bed and the room. Then she brought him a bowl of chicken broth with which she fed him. It tasted delicious, and he swallowed it hungrily and wished there had been more. Then as he lay back on the pillows he remembered all that had happened--the horses running down the street, his attempt to stop them, and the awful blow on his head as it struck the curbstone.

"Wonder where I am? Tain't a hospital, anyhow," he thought. "My! But I feel nice an' clean an' so--so light, somehow! If only my head wasn't so sore!"

No wonder he felt "nice and clean and light somehow," when, for the first time in his life his body and garments as well as his bed, were as sweet and fresh as hands could make them. Tode never had minded dirt. Why should he, when he had been born in it and had grown up knowing nothing better? Yet, none the less, was this new experience most delightful to him-- so delightful that he didn't care to talk. It was happiness enough for him, just then, to lie still and enjoy these new conditions, and so presently he floated off again into sleep--a sleep full of beautiful dreams from which the low murmur of voices aroused him, and he opened his eyes to see the nurse and the doctor looking down at him.

"Well, my boy," said the doctor, with his fingers on the wrist near him, "you look better. Feel better too, don't you?"

Tode gazed at him, wondering who he was and paying no attention to his question.

"Doctor," exclaimed the nurse, suddenly, "he hasn't spoken a single word. Do you suppose he can be deaf and dumb?"

The bishop entered the room just in time to catch the last words.

"Deaf and dumb!" he repeated, in a tone of dismay. "Dear me! If the poor child is deaf and dumb, I shall certainly keep him here until I can find a better home for him."

As his eyes rested on the bishop Tode started and uttered a little inarticulate cry of joy; then, as he understood what the bishop was saying, a singular expression passed over his face. The doctor, watching him closely could make nothing of it.

"He looks as if he knew you, bishop," the doctor said.

The bishop had taken the boy's rough little hand in his own large, kindly grasp.

"No, doctor," he answered, "I don't think I've ever seen him before yesterday, but we're friends all the same, aren't we, my lad?" and he smiled down into the grey eyes looking up to him so earnestly and happily.

Tode opened his lips to speak, then suddenly remembering, slightly shook his head while the colour mounted in his pale cheeks.

"He acts like a deaf mute, certainly," muttered the doctor, and stepping to the head of the bed he pulled out his watch and held it first to one and then the other of Tode's ears, but out of his sight.

Tode's ears were as sharp as a ferret's and his brain was as quick as his ears. He knew well enough what the doctor was doing but he made no sign. Were not the bishop's words ringing in his ears? "If the poor child is deaf and dumb I shall certainly keep him here until I can find a better home for him."

There were few things at which the boy would have hesitated to ensure his staying there. He understood now that he was in the house of the bishop-- "my bishop" he called him in his thought.

So, naturally enough, it was taken for granted that the boy was deaf and dumb, for no one imagined the possibility of his pretending to be so. Tode thought it would be easy to keep up the deception, but at first he found it very hard. As his strength returned there were so many questions that he wanted to ask, but he fully believed that if it were known that he could hear and speak he would be sent away, and more and more as the days went by he longed to remain where he was.

As he grew stronger and able to sit up, books and games and pictures were provided for his amusement, yet still the hours sometimes dragged somewhat heavily, but it was better when he was well enough to walk about the house.

Mrs. Martin, the housekeeper, had first admired the boy's bravery, then pitied him for his suffering, and had ended by loving him, because she, too, had a big, kindly heart that was ready to love anybody who needed her love and service. So, it was with great satisfaction that she obeyed the bishop's orders, and bought for the boy a good, serviceable outfit as soon as he was able to walk about his room.

She combed out and trimmed his rough, thick hair, and then helped him dress himself in one of his new suits. As she tied his necktie for him she looked at him with the greatest satisfaction, saying to herself,

"Whoever would believe that it was the same boy? If only he could hear and speak now like other boys, I'd have nothing more to ask for him."

Then she stooped and kissed him. Tode wriggled uneasily under the unwonted caress, not quite certain whether or not he liked it--from a woman. The housekeeper took his hand and led him down the stairs to the bishop's study. It was a long room containing many books and easy-chairs and two large desks. At one of these the bishop sat writing, and over the other bent a short, dark-faced man who wore glasses.

"Come in, Mrs. Martin, come in," called the bishop, as he saw her standing at the open door. "And who is this?" he added, holding out his hand to the boy.

"You don't recognize him?" Mrs. Martin asked smiling down on Tode's smooth head.

The bishop looked keenly at the boy, then he smiled contentedly and drew the little fellow to his side.

"Well, well!" he said, "the clothes we wear do make a great difference, don't they, Mrs. Martin? He's a fine looking lad. Gibson, this is the boy I was telling you about."

The little dark man turned and looked at Tode as the bishop spoke. It was not a friendly look, and Tode felt it.

"Ah," replied Mr. Gibson, slowly. "So this is the boy, is it? He was fortunate to fall into your hands;" and with a sharp, sidelong glance over his shoulder, Mr. Gibson turned again to his work.

The bishop drew a great armchair close to his table and gently pushed Tode into it. Then he brought a big book full of pictures and put it into the boy's hands.

"Let him stay here for a while, Mrs. Martin," he said. "I always work better when there is a child near me--if it's the right sort of a child," he added, with a smile.

Mrs. Martin went out, and Tode, with a long, happy breath, leaned back in the big chair and looked about him at the many books, at the dark head bent over the desk in the alcove, finally at the noble face of the bishop intent on his writing.

This was the beginning of many happy hours for Tode. Perhaps it was the weakness and languor resulting from his accident that made him willing to sit quietly a whole morning or afternoon in the study beside the bishop's table, when, before this, to sit still for half an hour would have been an almost unendurable penance to him; but there was another and a far stronger reason in the deep reverential love for the bishop, that day by day was growing and strengthening into a passion in his young heart. The boy's heart was like a garden-spot in which the rich, strong soil lay ready to receive any seed that might fall upon it. Better seed could not be than that which all unconsciously this man of God--the bishop--was sowing therein, as day after day he gave his Master's message to the sick and sinful and sorrowful souls that came to him for help and comfort.

It goes without saying that the bishop had small leisure, for many and heavy were the demands upon his time and thought, but nevertheless he kept two hours a day sacredly free from all other claims, that he might give them to any of God's poor or troubled ones who desired to see him, and believing that Tode could hear nothing that was said, he often kept the boy with him during these hours.

Strange and wonderful lessons were those that the little street boy learned from the consecrated lips of the good bishop--lessons of God's love to man, and of the loving service that man owes not only to his God, but to his brother man. Strange, sad lessons too, of sin and sorrow, and their far-reaching influence on human lives. Tode had not lived in the streets for nearly fourteen years without learning a great deal about the sin that is in the world, but never until now, had he understood and realised the evil of it and the cure for it. Many a time he longed to ask the bishop some of the questions that filled his mind, but that he dared not do.

Among these visitors there came one morning to the study a plainly dressed lady with a face that Tode liked at the first glance. As she talked with the bishop, the boy kept his eyes on the book open in his lap, but he heard all that was said--heard it at first with a startled surprise that changed into a sick feeling of shame and misery--for the story to which he listened was this:

The lady was a Mrs. Russell. The bishop had formerly been her pastor and she still came to him for help and counsel. She had been much interested in a boy of sixteen who had been in her class in the mission school, a boy who was entirely alone in the world. He had picked up a living in the streets, much as Tode himself had done, and finally had fallen into bad company and into trouble.

Mrs. Russell had interested herself in his behalf, and upon her promise to be responsible for him, he had been delivered over to her instead of being sent to a reform school. She went to a number of the smaller dry goods stores and secured promises of employment for the boy as parcel deliverer. To do this work he must have a tricycle, and the energetic little lady having found a secondhand one that could be had for thirty dollars, set herself to secure this sum from several of her friends. This she had done, and was on her way to buy the tricycle when she lost her pocketbook. The owner of the tricycle, being anxious to sell, and having another offer, would not hold it for her, but sold it to the other customer. The boy, bitterly disappointed, lost hope and heart, and that night left the place where Mrs. Russell had put him. Since then she had sought in vain for him, and now, unwilling to give him up, she had come to ask the bishop's help in the search.

To all this Tode listened with flushed cheeks and fast-beating heart, while before his mind flashed a picture of himself, wet, dirty and ragged, gliding under the feet of the horses on the muddy street, the missing pocketbook clutched tightly in his hand. Then a second picture rose before him, and he saw himself crowding the emptied book into that box on the chapel door of St. Mark's.

The bishop pulled open a drawer in his desk and took from it a pocketbook, broken and stained with mud. He handed it to Mrs. Russell, who looked at him in silent wonder as she saw her own name on the inside.

"How did it get into your hands?" she questioned, at last.

"You would never guess how," the bishop answered. "It was found in the pastor's box at St. Mark's, and the rector came to me to inquire if I knew any one of that name. I had not your present address, but have been intending to look you up as soon as I could find time."

"I cannot understand it," said Mrs. Russell, carefully examining each compartment of the book. "Why in the world should the thief have put the empty pocketbook there, of all places?"

"Of course he would want to get rid of it," the bishop replied, thoughtfully, "but that certainly was a strange place in which to put it."

"If the thief could know how the loss of that money drove that poor foolish boy back into sin and misery, he surely would wish he had never touched it--if he has any conscience left," said Mrs. Russell. "There is good stuff in that poor boy of mine, and I can't bear to give him up and leave him to go to ruin."

The bishop looked at her with a grave smile as he answered:

"Mrs. Russell, I never yet knew you willing to give up one of your straying lambs. Like the Master Himself, your big heart always yearns over the wanderers from the fold. I wonder," he added, "if we couldn't get one or two newsboys to help in this search. Many of them are very keen, sharp little fellows, and they'd be as likely as anybody to know Jack, and to know his whereabouts if he is still in the city. Let me see--his name is Jack Finney, and he is about fifteen or sixteen now, isn't he?"

"Yes, nearly sixteen."

"Suppose you give me a description of him, Mrs. Russell. I ought to remember how he looks, but I see so many, you know," the bishop added, apologetically.

"Of course you cannot remember all the boys who were in our mission school," replied Mrs. Russell. "Jack is tall and large, for fifteen. His hair is sandy, his eyes blue, and, well--his mouth is rather large. Jack isn't a beauty, and he is rough and rude, and I'm afraid he often does things that he ought not to do, but only think what a hard time he has had in the world thus far."

"Yes," replied the bishop with a sigh, "he has had a hard time, and it is not to be wondered at that he has gone wrong. Many a boy does that who has every help toward right living. Well now, Mrs. Russell, I'll see what I can do to help you in this matter. Your faith in the boy ought to go far toward keeping him straight if we can find him."

The bishop walked to the hall with his visitor. When he came back Tode sat with his eyes fastened on the open book in his lap, though he saw it not.

He did not look up with his usual bright smile when the bishop sat down beside him. That night he could not eat, and when he went to bed he could not sleep.

"Thief! Thief! You're a thief! You're a thief!"

Over and over and over again these words sounded in Tode's ears. He had known of course that he was a thief, but he had never realised it until this day. As he had sat there and listened to Mrs. Russell's story, he seemed to see clearly how his soul had been soiled with sin as surely as his body had been with dirt, and even as now the thought of going back to his former surroundings sickened him, so the remembrance of the evil that he had known and done, now seemed horrible to him. It was as if he looked at himself and his past life through the pure eyes of the bishop--and he hated it all. Dimly he began to see that there was something that he must do, but what that something was, he could not as yet determine. He was not willing in fact to do what his newly awakened conscience told him that he ought to do.

In the morning he showed so plainly the effects of his wakeful night, and of his first moral battle, that the bishop was much concerned.

He had begun to teach the boy to write that he might communicate with him in that fashion, but as yet Tode had not progressed far enough to make communication with him easy, though he was beginning to read quite readily the bold, clear handwriting of the bishop.

This morning, the bishop, noting the boy's pale cheeks and heavy eyes, proposed a walk instead of the writing lesson. Tode was delighted to go, and the two set off together. Now the boy had an opportunity to see yet farther into the heart and life of this good, great man. They went on and on, away from the wide streets and handsome houses, into the tenement house district, and finally into an old building, where many families found shelter--such as it was. Up one flight after another of rickety stairs the bishop led the boy. At last he stopped and knocked at a door on a dark landing.

The door was opened by a woman whose eyes looked as if she had forgotten how to smile, but a light flashed into them at sight of her visitor. She hurriedly dusted a chair with her apron, and as the bishop took it he lifted to his knee one of the little ones clinging to the mother's skirts. There were four little children, but one lay, pale and motionless on a bed in one corner of the room.

"She is sick?" inquired the bishop, his voice full of sympathy, as he looked at the small, wan face.

The woman's eyes filled with tears.

"Yes," she answered, "I doubt I'm goin' to lose her, an' I feel I ought to be glad for her sake--but I can't." She bent over the little form and kissed the heavy eyelids.

"Tell me all about it, my daughter," the bishop said, and the woman poured out her story--the old story of a husband who provided for his family after a fashion, when he was sober, but left them to starve when the drink demon possessed him. He had been away now for three weeks, and there was no money for medicine for the sick child, or food for the others.

Before the story was told the bishop's hand was in his pocket and he held out some money to the woman, saying,

"Go out and buy what you need. It will be better for you to get it, than for me to. The breath of air will do you good, and I will see to the children until you come back."

She hesitated for a moment, then with a word of thanks, threw a shawl over her head and was gone.

The bishop gathered the three older children about him, one on each knee and the third held close to his side, and told them stories that held them spellbound until the sick baby began to stir and moan feebly. Then the bishop arose, and taking the little creature tenderly in his strong arms, walked back and forth in the small room until the moaning cry ceased and the child slept. He had just laid it again on the bed when the mother came back with her arms full of packages. The look of dull despair was gone from her worn face, and there was a gleam of hope in her eyes as she hastily prepared the medicine for the baby, while the bishop eagerly tore open one of the packages, and put bread into the hands of the other children.

"God bless you, sir,--an' He will!" the woman said, earnestly, as the bishop was departing with a promise to come soon again.

Tode, from his seat in a corner had looked on and listened to all, and now followed the bishop down to the street, and on until they came to a big building. The boy did not know then what place it was. Afterward he learned that it was the poorhouse.

Among the human driftwood gathered here there was one old man who had been a cobbler, working at his trade as long as he had strength to do so. The bishop had known him for a long time before he gave up his work, and now it was the one delight of the old man's life to have a visit from the bishop, and knowing this, the latter never failed to come several times each year. The old cobbler lived on the memory of these visits through the lonely weeks that followed them, looking forward to them as the only bright spots in his sorrowful life.

"You'll pray with me before ye go?" he pleaded on this day when his visitor arose to leave.

"Surely," was the quick reply, and the bishop, falling on his knees, drew Tode down beside him, and the old cobbler, the child and the man of God, bowed their heads together.

A great wonder fell upon Tode first, as he listened to that prayer, and then his heart seemed to melt within him. When he rose from his knees, he had learned Who and What God is, and what it is to pray, and though he could not understand how it was, or why--he knew that henceforth his own life must be wholly different. Something in him was changed and he was full of a strange happiness as he walked homeward beside his friend.

But all in a moment his new joy departed, banished by the remembrance of that pocketbook.

"I found it. I picked it up," he argued to himself, but then arose before him the memory of other things that he had stolen--of many an evil thing that

63

he had done, and gloried in the doing. Now the remembrance of these things made him wretched.

The bishop was to deliver an address that evening, and Tode was alone, for he did not feel like going to the housekeeper's room.

He was free to go where he chose about the house, so he wandered from room to room, and finally to the study. It was dark there, but he felt his way to his seat beside the bishop's desk, and sitting there in the dark the boy faced his past and his future; faced, too, a duty that lay before him--a duty so hard that it seemed to him he never could perform it, yet he knew he must. It was to tell the bishop how he had been deceiving him all these weeks.

Tears were strangers to Tode's eyes, but they flowed down his cheeks as he sat there in the dark and thought of the happy days he had spent there, and that now he must go away from it all--away from the bishop--back to the wretched and miserable life which was all he had known before.

"Oh, how can I tell him! How can I tell him!" he sobbed aloud, with his head on the desk.

The next moment a strong, wiry hand seized his right ear with a grip that made him wince, while a voice with a thrill of evil satisfaction in it, exclaimed in a low, guarded tone,

"So! I've caught you, you young cheat. I've suspected for some time that you were pulling the wool over the bishop's eyes, but you were so plaguy cunning that I couldn't nab you before. You're a fine specimen, aren't you? What do you think the bishop will say to all this?"

Tode had recognised the voice of Mr. Gibson, the secretary. He knew that the secretary had a way of going about as soft-footed as a cat. He tried to jerk his ear free, but at that Mr. Gibson gave it such a tweak that Tode could hardly keep from crying out with the pain. He did keep from it, however, and the next moment the secretary let him go, and, striking a match, lit the gas, and then softly closed the door.

"Now," he said, coming back to the desk, "what have you to say for yourself?"

"Nothing--to you," replied Tode, looking full into the dark face and cruel eyes of the man. "I'll tell the bishop myself what there is to tell."

"Oh, you will, will you?" answered the man, with a sneer. "I reckon before you get through with your telling you'll wish you'd never been born. The bishop's the gentlest of men--until he finds that some one has been trying to deceive him. And you--you whom he picked up out of the street, you whom he has treated as if you were his own son--I tell you, boy, you'll think you've been struck by lightning when the bishop orders you out of his sight. He never forgives deceit like yours."

Tode's face paled and his lips trembled as he listened, but he would not give way before his tormentor.

His silence angered the secretary yet more. "Why don't you speak?" he exclaimed, sharply.

"I'll speak to the bishop--not to you," replied the boy, steadily.

His defiant tone and undaunted look made the secretary furious. He sprang toward the boy, but Tode was on the watch now, and slipped out of his chair and round to the other side of the desk, where he stopped and again faced his enemy, for he knew now that this man was his enemy, though he could not guess the reason of his enmity. The secretary took a step forward, but at that Tode sped across the room out of the door, and up to his own room, the door of which he locked.

Then he sat down and thought over what had happened, and the more he thought of it the more certain he felt that what the secretary had said was true.

A long, long time the boy sat there, thinking sad and bitter thoughts. At last, with a heavy sigh, he lifted his head and looked about the bright, pretty room, as if he would fix it all in his mind so that he never could forget it, and as he looked at the soft, rich carpet, the little white bed with its fresh, clean linen, the wide, roomy washstand and bureau, he seemed at the same time to see the bare, dirty, cheerless little closet-like room to which he must return, and his heart ached again.

At last he started up, searched in his pockets for a piece of paper and a pencil, and began to write. His paper was a much-crumpled piece that he had found that morning in the wastebasket, and as yet his writing and spelling were poor enough, but he knew what he wanted to express, and this is what he wrote:

DEAR BISHOP:

I hav ben mene and bad i am not def and dum but i acted like i was caus I thot you wood not kepe me if yu knu I am sory now so i am going away but i am going to kepe strate and not bee bad any more ever. I thank you and i lov you deer.

TODE BRYAN.

It took the boy a long time to write this and there were many smudges and erasures where he had rubbed out and rewritten words. He looked at it with dissatisfied eyes when it was done, mentally contrasting it with the neat, beautifully written letters he had so often seen on the bishop's desk.

"Can't help it. I can't do no better," he said to himself, with a sigh. Then he stood for several minutes holding the paper thoughtfully in his hand.

"I know," he exclaimed at last, and ran softly down to the study. It was dark again there and he knew that Mr. Gibson had gone.

Going to the desk, he found the Bible which the bishop always kept there. As Tode lifted it the leaves fell apart at one of the bishop's best-loved chapters, and there the boy laid his letter and closed the book. He hesitated a moment, and then kneeling down beside the desk, he laid his face on the cover of the Bible and whispered solemnly,

"I will keep straight--I will."

It was nearly nine o'clock when Tode returned to what had been his room; what would be so no longer. He undressed slowly, and as he took off each garment he looked at it and touched it lingeringly before he laid it aside.

"I b'lieve he'd want me to keep these clothes," he thought, "but I don't know. Maybe he wouldn't when he finds out how I've been cheatin' him. Mrs. Martin's burnt up my old ones, an' I've got to have some to wear, but I'll only take what I must have."

So, with a sigh, he laid aside his white shirt with its glossy collar and cuffs, his pretty necktie and handkerchief. He hesitated over the shoes and stockings, but finally with a shake of the head, those, too, were laid aside, leaving nothing but one under garment and his jacket, trousers and cap.

Then he put out the gas and crept into bed. A little later he heard Mrs. Martin go up to her room, stopping for a moment to glance into his and see that he was in bed. Later still, he heard the bishop come in and go to his room, and soon after the lights were out and all the house was still.

Tode lay with wide open eyes until the big hall clock struck twelve. Then he arose, slipped on his few garments and turned to leave the room, but suddenly went back and took up a little Testament.

"He told me to keep it always an' read a bit in it ev'ry day," the boy thought, as with the little book in his hand he crept silently down the stairs. They creaked under the light tread of his bare feet as they never had creaked in the daytime. He crossed the wide hall, unfastened the door, and passed out into the night.

VI. TODE'S NEW START

A chill seemed to strike to Tode's heart as he stood on the stone steps and looked up to the windows of the room where the bishop was sleeping, and his eyes were wet as he passed slowly and sorrowfully out of the gate and turned down the street. Suddenly there was a swift rush, a quick, joyful bark, and there was Tag, dancing about him, jumping up to lick his fingers, and altogether almost out of his wits with joy.

Tode sat down on the curbstone and hugged his rough, faithful friend, and if he whispered into the dog's ear some of the grief that made the hour such a bitter one--Tag was true and trusty: he never told it. Neither did he tell how, night after night, he had watched beside the big house into which he had seen his master carried, nor how many times he had been driven away in the morning by the servants. But Tag's troubles were over now. He had found his master.

"Well, ol' fellow, we can't stay here all night. We must go on," Tode said at last, and the two walked on together to the house where the boy had slept before his accident. The outer door was ajar as usual, and Tode and the dog went up the stairs together.

Tode tried the door of his room. It was locked on the inside.

"They've let somebody else have it," he said to himself. "Well, Tag, we'll have to find some other place. Come on!"

Once the boy would not have minded sleeping on a grating, or a doorstep, but now it seemed hard and dreary enough to him. He shivered with the cold and shrank from going to any of his old haunts where he would be likely to find some of his acquaintances, homeless street Arabs, like himself. Finally he found an empty packing box in an alley, and into this he crept, glad to put his bare feet against Tag's warm body. But it was a dreary night to him, and weary as he was, he slept but little. As he lay there looking up at the stars, he thought much of the new life that he was to live henceforth. He knew very well that it would be no easy thing for him to live such a life, but obstacles in his way never deterred Tode from doing, or at least attempting to do, what he had made up his mind to. He thought much, too, of the bishop, and these thoughts gave him such a heartache that he would almost have banished them had he been able to do so-- almost, but not quite, for even with the heartache it was a joy to him to recall every look of that noble face--every tone of that voice that seemed to thrill his heart even in the remembrance.

Then came thoughts of Nan and Little Brother, and these brought comfort to Tode's sorrowful heart. He had not forgotten Little Brother during the past weeks. There had never been a day when he had not thought of the child with a longing desire to see him, though even for his sake he could hardly have brought himself to lose a day with the bishop. Now, however, that he had shut himself out forever from what seemed to him the Paradise of the bishop's home, his thoughts turned again lovingly toward the little one, and he could hardly wait for morning, so eager was he to go to him.

Fortunately for his impatience, he knew that the Hunts and Nan would be early astir, and at the first possible moment he went in search of them. He ran up the stairs with Tag at his heels, and almost trembling with eagerness, knocked at the Hunts' door. Mrs. Hunt herself opened it, and stared at the boy for a moment before she realised who it was.

"For the land's sake, if it isn't Tode! Where in the world have you been all this time?" she cried, holding the door open for him to enter, while the children gazed wonderingly at him. "I've been sick--got hurt," replied Tode, his eyes searching eagerly about the room. "I don't see Nan or Little Brother," he added, uneasily.

"They don't live here no more," piped up little Ned.

Tode turned a startled glance upon Mrs. Hunt.

"Don't live here!" he stammered. "Where do they live?"

"Not far off; just cross the entry," replied Mrs. Hunt, quickly. "Nan's taken a room herself."

"Oh!" cried Tode, in a tone of relief, "I'll go'n see her;" and waiting for no further words, he went.

"Well," exclaimed Mrs. Hunt, "he might 'a' told us how he got hurt an' all, 'fore he rushed off, I should think."

"Jus' like that Tode Bryan. He don't know nothin'!" remarked Dick, scornfully.

His mother gave him a searching glance. "There's worse boys than Tode Bryan, I'm afraid," she said.

"There ye go agin, always a flingin' at me," retorted Dick, rudely. "How's a feller to git on in the world when his own mother's always down on him?"

"You know I'm not down on you, Dick," replied his mother, tearfully.

"You're always a hintin' nowdays, anyhow," muttered Dick, as he reached over and helped himself to the biggest sausage in the dish.

Mrs. Hunt sighed but made no answer, and the breakfast was eaten mostly in silence.

Meantime, Tode running across the entry, had knocked on the door with fingers fairly trembling with eagerness and excitement. Nan opening it, gave a glad cry at sight of him, but the boy, with a nod, pushed by her, and snatched up Little Brother who was lying on the bed.

The baby stared at him for an instant and then as Tode hugged him more roughly than he realised, the little lips trembled and the baby began to sob. That almost broke Tode's heart. He put the child down, crying out bitterly,

"Oh Little Brother, you ain't goin' to turn against me, sure?"

As he spoke he held out his hands wistfully, and the baby, now getting a good look at him, recognised his favorite, and with his old smile held out his arms to the boy, who caught him up again but more gently this time, and sat down with him on his knee.

It was some minutes before Tode paid any attention to Nan's questions, so absorbed was he with the child, but at length he turned to her and told her where he had been and what had happened to him. She listened to his story with an eager interest that pleased him.

"Wasn't it strange," she said, when he paused, "wasn't it strange, and lovely too, that you should have been taken into the bishop's house--and kept there all this time? Did you like him just as much in his home as in the church, Tode?"

"He's--he's"--began Tode with shining eyes, then as the bishop's face rose before him, he choked and was silent for a moment. "I don't b'lieve there's any other man like him in thisworld," he said, finally.

Nan looked at him thoughtfully, at his face that seemed to have been changed and refined by his sickness and his new associations, at the neat clothes he wore, then at his bare feet.

"I shouldn't think, if he's so good, that he would have let you come away--so," she said, slowly.

Tode flushed as he tried to hide his feet under his chair.

"'Twasn't his fault," he answered, quickly. He too was silent for a moment, then suddenly he sat upright with a look of stern resolve in his grey eyes, as he added, "Nan, I'll tell you all there is about it, 'cause things are goin' to be diff'runt after this. I'm goin' to live straight every way, I am; I've--promised."

Then he told her frankly the whole story; how he had deceived the bishop, pretending to be deaf and dumb; how Mr. Gibson had come upon him in the study, and what he had said, and how, finally, he himself had come away in the night.

Nan listened to it all with the keenest interest.

"And you had to sleep out of doors," she said; "I'm so sorry, but, if the bishop is so good, why didn't you stay and tell him all about it, Tode?

Don't you think that that would have been better than coming away so without thanking him for all he had done--or anything?"

Tode shook his head emphatically. "You don't know him, Nan," he replied. "He's good, oh better than anybody else in the world, I b'lieve, but don't you see, just 'cause he's so good, he hates cheatin' an' lyin', just hates 'em; an', oh I couldn't tell him I'd been cheatin' him all this time, an' he so good to me."

"I know, 'twould have been awful hard to tell him, Tode, but seems to me 'twould have been best," the girl insisted.

"I couldn't, Nan," Tode repeated, sadly, then impatiently thrusting aside his sorrow and remorse, he added,

"Come now, I want to know what you've been doin' while I've been gone. I used to think an' think 'bout you'n him," glancing at the baby, "an' wonder what you'd be doin'."

"Oh, we've got on all right," answered Nan, "I was worried enough when you didn't come, 'specially when one of the Hunt boys went down and found that your stand had not been opened. I was sure something had happened to you, 'cause I knew you never would stay away from us so, unless something was the matter."

"Right you are!" put in Tode, emphatically.

Nan went on, "I was sure there was something wrong, too, when Tag came here the next day. Poor fellow, I was so sorry for him. One of his legs was all swollen and he limped dreadfully, and hungry--why, Tode, he acted as if he were starving. But just as soon as I had fed him he went off again, and didn't come back till the next morning, and he's done that way ever since."

Tag had kept his bright eyes fastened on Nan's face while she talked, and he gave a little contented whine as Tode stooped and patted his head.

"But tell me what you've ben doin', Nan. How'd you get money enough to hire this room an' fix it up so dandy?" Tode inquired, looking about admiringly.

While Nan talked she had been passing busily from table to stove, and now she said, "Breakfast is ready, Tode. Bring your chair up here and give me Little Brother."

Tode reluctantly gave up the baby, and took his seat opposite Nan at the little table.

"You've got things fine," he remarked, glancing at the clean towel that served for a tablecloth, and the neat white dishes and well-cooked food. He was hungry enough to do full justice to Nan's cooking, and the girl watched him with much satisfaction, eating little herself, but feeding the baby, as she went on with her story.

"When you didn't come back, I knew I must find some way to sell my cookies and gingerbread and so I made some fresh and went to every family in this house and asked 'em if they would buy their bread and all of me instead of at the bakeshops. I told 'em I'd sell at the same price as the shops and give them better things. Some wouldn't, but most of them had sense enough to see that it would be a good thing for them, and after they'd tried it once or twice they were ready enough to keep on. Now I supply this house and the next one. It keeps me cooking all day, but I don't mind that. I'm only too glad that I can earn our living--Little Brother's and mine. Of course, I couldn't be cooking all day on Mrs. Hunt's stove, and besides they have no room to spare and we crowded 'em, and so, as soon as I got money enough, I hired this room. I'm paying for the furniture as fast as I can. It was all secondhand, of course."

Tode looked admiringly at the girl, as she ceased speaking.

"You've got a head," he remarked. "But now about cooking for my stand. Will you have time to do that too?"

"Yes indeed," replied Nan, promptly. "I'll find time somehow."

Tode hesitated, moved uneasily in his chair and finally said, "'Spect you'll have to trust me for the first lot, Nan. I ain't got no money, ye know."

"Why, Tode, have you forgotten that ten dollars you asked me to keep for you?"

"No--'course I ain't forgot it, but I thought maybe you'd had to use it. Twould 'a' been all right if you had, you know."

"Oh no, I didn't have to use that. Here it is," and Nan brought it out from some hidden pocket about her dress.

"Then I'm all right," exclaimed the boy, in a tone of satisfaction. "I've got to get some clothes first an' then I'll be ready for business."

"What's the matter with those clothes?" questioned Nan.

"Oh, I've got to send these back to the bishop." Tode's face was grave as he spoke.

"But--I don't see why. He won't want em," Nan remonstrated.

"It's this way, Nan." Tode spoke very earnestly. "If I'd been what he thought I was, I know I could have kept all he gave me, but, you see, if he'd known I was cheatin' an' lyin' to him all the time he wouldn't 'a' given me a single thing, so don't ye see, I ain't no business to keep 'em, an' I ain't goin' to keep 'em a minute longer'n I have to."

Nan shook her head, for Tode's reasoning had not convinced her, but seeing how strong was his feeling in the matter she said no more, and in a few minutes the boy went out, his face radiant with satisfaction, because Little Brother cried after him.

He invested half his ten dollars in some second-hand clothes, including shoes and stockings. They were not very satisfactory after the garments he had been wearing of late, but he said to himself, "They'll have to do till I can get better ones an' sometime I'm agoin' to have some shirts an' have 'em washed every week, too."

Tode's trade, that day, was not very heavy, for it was not yet known among his regular customers that he had reopened his stand, but he took care to advertise the fact through those whom he met and he did not fear but that his business would soon be prospering again.

That afternoon he succeeded in securing a tiny room in the house with Nan. It was a dismal little closet, lighted only from the hall, but it was the best he could do, and Tode considered himself fortunate to have his dark corner to himself, even though a broken chair and a canvas cot without bedding of any sort were all the furniture he could put into it then. Nan shook her head doubtfully when he showed her the room.

"Dark and dirty," she said, with a sniff of disgust, as the boy threw open the door. "You must get somebody to scrub it for you, Tode, and then whitewash the walls. That will make it sweeter and lighter."

"So it will," responded the boy, promptly, "but I'll have to do the scrubbin' an' white-washin' both, myself."

Nan looked at him doubtfully. "I wonder if you'd get it clean," she said. "Scrubbing's hard work."

"You'll see. What'll I scrub it with--a broom?"

"You ought to have a scrub-brush, but I haven't any. You'll have to do it with an old broom and a cloth. I can let you have the broom and I guess we can get a cloth of Mrs. Hunt. You going to do it now?" she added, as Tode began to pull off his coat.

"Right now," he answered. "You see, Nan, I've got loads of things to do, an' I can't be wastin' time."

"What things?" questioned Nan, curiously.

"Oh--I'll tell you about them after awhile," replied the boy. "The broom in your room?"

"Yes, I'll bring it to you," and Nan hurried off.

She came back with an old pail full of hot water, a piece of soap, a broom and a cloth, and then she proceeded to show Tode how to clean the woodwork and floor, thoroughly, with special attention to the dark corners which looked, indeed, as if they had never been visited by a broom. Nan was a thorough little housewife, and she longed to do the whole work herself, but Tode would not allow that, so she could only stand and look on, wondering inwardly how a boy could handle a broom so awkwardly. But if he was slow and awkward about it, Tode was in earnest, and he looked with much satisfaction at the result of his labor when it was completed.

"You'll have to wash the floor again after you've whitewashed the walls," Nan said, "but it needed two scrubbings, anyhow."

Tode looked at it ruefully. "Oh, did it?" he said. "I think one such scrubbing as that ought to last it a year."

Nan laughed. "If you'll carry out my bread and things to-morrow, I'll do your whitewashing for you," she said.

But Tode shook his head. "I'll carry out your stuff all right," he answered, "but I ain't a-goin' to have a girl doin' my work for me."

He bought the lime and paid also for the use of a pail and brush, and the next day he put a white coat on his walls, and when this was done, he was much better satisfied with his quarters. Nan offered to lend him her shawl in place of a blanket, but he guessed that she needed it herself and refused her offer.

VII. AFTER TODE'S DEPARTURE

In the bishop's household, Mrs. Martin was always one of the earliest to rise in the morning, and just as Tode sat down to breakfast with Nan and Little Brother, the housekeeper was going downstairs. Tode's door stood open and she saw that he was not in the room. Her quick eyes noted also the pile of neatly folded garments on a chair beside the bed. She stepped into the room and looked around. Then she hurried to the study, knowing that the boy loved to stay there, but the study was unoccupied.

By the time breakfast was ready she knew that the boy had left the house, but the bishop refused to believe it, nor would he be convinced until the house had been searched from attic to cellar. When Mr. Gibson made his appearance, a gleam of satisfaction shone in his narrow eyes as he learned of Tode's disappearance.

"I was afraid something like this would happen," he remarked, gravely. "It's a hopeless kind of business, trying to make anything out of such material. I've had my suspicions of that boy for some time."

"Don't be too quick to condemn him, Mr. Gibson," exclaimed the bishop, hastily. "He may have had some good reason for going away so. I've no doubt he thought he had, but I had grown to love the lad and I shall miss him sadly."

"Did you never suspect that he was not deaf and dumb, as he pretended to be?" the secretary asked.

The bishop looked up quickly. "Why, no, indeed, I never had such an idea," he answered. An unpleasant smile flickered over the secretary's thin lips as he went on, "I heard the boy talking to himself, here in this room, last evening. He can hear and speak as well as you or I."

"Oh, I am sorry! I am sorry!" said the bishop, sadly, and then he turned to his desk, and sitting down, hid his face in his hands, and was silent. The secretary cast more than one swift, sidewise glance at him, but dared say no more then.

After a while the bishop drew his Bible toward him. It opened at the fourteenth chapter of John, and there lay Tode's poor little soiled and blotted note. The bishop read it with tear-dimmed eyes, read it again and again, and finally slipped it into an envelope, and replaced it between the leaves of his Bible. He said nothing about it to his secretary, and presently he went to his own room, where for a long time he walked back and forth, thinking about the boy, and how he might find him again.

Then Brown came to him with a telegram summoning him to the sickbed of his only sister, and within an hour he left the city, and was absent two weeks.

Meantime Tode, the morning after his scrubbing and whitewashing operations, had carefully folded the clothes he had worn when he left the bishop's house and tied them up in an old newspaper. Into one of the pockets of the jacket he had put a note which ran thus:

DEAR MRS. MARTIN:

Pleas giv thes cloes to the bishop and tell him i wud not have took them away if i had had any others. I did not take shoes or stockins. I keep the littel testament and i read in it evry day. Tell him i am trying to be good and when i get good enuf I shall go and see him. You was good to me but he was so good that he made me hate myself and evrything bad. I can never be bad again while i remember him.

TODE BRYAN.

He hired a boy whom he knew, to carry the bundle to the bishop's house, and from behind a tree-box further down the street, he watched and saw it taken in by Brown. The boy's heart was beating hard and fast, as he stood there longing, yet dreading, to see the bishop himself come out of the house. But the bishop was far away, and Tode walked sadly homeward, casting many a wistful, lingering glance backward, as he went.

Brown carried the package gingerly to Mrs. Martin, for the boy who had delivered it was not over clean, and Mrs. Martin opened it with some suspicion, but when she saw the clothes she recognised them instantly, and finding the note in the pocket read it with wet eyes.

"I knew that wasn't a bad boy," she said to herself, "and this proves it. He's as honest as the day, or he wouldn't have sent back these clothes--the poor little fellow. Well, well! I hope the bishop can find him when he gets back, and as to the boy's pretending to be deaf and dumb, I'm sure there was something underneath that if we only knew it. Anyhow, I do hope I'll see the little fellow again sometime."

When the bishop returned the accumulated work of his weeks of absence so pressed upon him that for a while he had no time for anything else, and when at last he was free to search for Tode, he could find no trace of him.

As for Tode, he had never once thought of the possibility of the bishop's searching for him. He looked forward to seeing his friend again sometime, but that time he put far away when he himself should be "more fit," as he said to himself.

One evening soon after his return, Nan had a long talk with him, a talk that left her wondering greatly at the change in his thoughts and purposes, and which made her regard him with quite a new feeling of respect.

"Nan," he began, "I told you I'd got loads of things to do now."

"Yes?" The girl looked at him inquiringly.

Tode was silent for a little. It was harder for him to speak than he had thought it would be.

"You see," he went on, slowly, "I've been mean as dirt all my life. You don't know what mean things I've done, an' I ain't goin' to tell ye, only that I know now I've got to turn straight around an' not do 'em any more. I've got to make a man of myself," he drew himself up as he spoke, "a real man--the kind that helps other folks up. I can't say just what I mean, but I feel it myself," he added, with a half-appealing glance at Nan.

She had listened attentively with her eyes fastened on his earnest face. Now she said softly, "You mean--you want to be the kind of man the bishop is, don't you?"

"Oh, I couldn't ever be really like him," protested the boy, quickly, "but, well, I'm goin' to try to be a sort of shadow of him. I mean I'm goin' to try to amount to something myself, an' do what I can to help other poor fellers up instead of down. I'm goin' to lend a hand 'mongst the folks 'round here, just a little you know, as he does 'mongst the poor people he goes to see. But I've got some other things to do too. I've got some money to pay back, an' I've got to find a feller that I helped to pull down."

And thereupon, Tode told the story of Mrs. Russell's pocketbook and her search for Jack Finney. He told it all quite frankly, not trying in the least to excuse or lessen his own guilt in the matter.

"It will take you a long time to save up so much money, Tode," Nan said when he paused.

"Yes, unless I can find some way to earn more, but I can't help that. I'll do the best I can, an' I've got some notions in my head."

He talked over with her some of his plans and projects, and as she listened, she thought to herself, "He's getting 'way ahead of me, but I'm afraid he'll get into trouble at first."

And she was not mistaken. Tode was now so thoroughly in earnest himself that he forgot to take into consideration the fact that those whom he meant to help up might prefer to be left to go down in their own fashion. His old associates speedily discovered that a great change had come over Tode Bryan, and the change did not meet with their approval. They called it "mighty cheeky" of him to be "pokin' his nose" into their affairs, and they would show him that he'd better stop it. So Tode soon found himself exceedingly unpopular, and, what was worse, in a way, under a boycott that threatened to ruin his business.

He fell into the way of carrying his trials and perplexities to Nan, and talking them over with her. She had plenty of that common sense, which is not very common after all, and she often made him see the reason of his failures, while at the same time he was sure of her sympathy.

One evening Tode appeared in her room with his little Testament in his hand. There was a perplexed expression in his eyes as he said, "Nan, 'bout readin' this, you know--I've been peggin' away at the first part, an' I can't make nothin' of it. It's just a string of funny words, names, I s'pose. I don't see no sense to it."

Nan glanced at the page to which he had opened. It was the first chapter of Matthew.

"Oh, that's all it is, just a lot of names. You can skip all that, Tode," she answered, easily.

"No I can't, neither," replied the boy, decidedly. "If I begin to skip, no knowin' where I'll stop. If it's readin' this book that makes folks good, I've got to know all 'bout it. Say, can't you read this with me an' tell me how to call all these jawbreakers?"

Nan looked rather shocked at the boy's free and easy reference to the Book, but seeing from his grave face and serious manner that he was very much in earnest, she sat down with him, and the two young heads bent over the page together.

"I remember reading this chapter with mother," Nan said, gently, "and she told me how to pronounce these names, but I can't remember all of them now. I'll do the best I can, though," and she read slowly the first seventeen verses, Tode repeating each name after her.

"Whew!" he exclaimed, in a tone of intense relief, when the task was ended, "that's 'bout the toughest job ever I tackled."

"Well, you see, you needn't read all that again. The rest of the chapter is different. It's all about Jesus," Nan said.

Tode read the remaining verses slowly by himself, but he shook his head in a dissatisfied way as he closed the book. "That's easier than the names to read, but I don't seem to get much out of it. Guess I'm too thick-headed," he said, in a discouraged tone.

"Tode," exclaimed Nan, suddenly, "you ought to go to some Sunday-school. Then you'd learn all about the Bible and the things you want to know."

"Might be a good scheme, that's a fact," he answered, thoughtfully. "Reckon I'll try it on anyhow, an' see how it works."

"Yes, do. I always used to go before mother was sick. If you have a good teacher you'll like it, I'm sure."

"There's a mission school down near my stand. I'll have a try at it next Sunday an' see what it's like," Tode said.

So the very next day he went to the mission chapel, and, from the notice on the door, found out the hours of service, and the following Sunday he was on hand in due season. As he went somewhat doubtfully up the steps, he saw in the vestibule a young man, who stepped forward and held out his hand, saying cordially,

"Glad to see you here. Are you a stranger?"

Tode wasn't quite sure what a stranger might be, but he muttered, "I ain't never been here before."

"Then I'm glad I happened to meet you. Will you come into my class?"

Tode nodded and followed the young man into the chapel, which was already nearly full of boys and girls.

"My name is Scott. What is yours?" inquired the stranger, as he led the way to his own corner of the room.

Tode gave his name, and Mr. Scott introduced him to half a dozen boys who had already taken their places in his class. One of these boys was Dick

Hunt. He gave Tode a careless nod by way of greeting, as the latter dropped into the seat next him.

To Tode's great satisfaction the lesson chanced to be on the birth of the Lord Jesus, and Mr. Scott told the boys the whole story so clearly and vividly, that Tode at least was intensely interested. It was all new and fresh to him, and he was listening eagerly to every word, when suddenly Dick Hunt ran a long pin deep into his leg. The pain made him start and almost cry out, but he suppressed the cry as he turned and gave Dick a savage pinch that made him writhe, as he exclaimed in a threatening tone, "You stop that!"

Mr. Scott turned grave, inquiring eyes on the two, as he asked:

"What's the matter, Dick?"

"He's a pinchin' me--Tode Bryan is. He give me an awful tweak when you wasn't a lookin'."

"Is that so?" Mr. Scott asked, and Tode, with a scornfully defiant glance at Dick, answered promptly, "Yes."

"I am sorry, Tode," said Mr. Scott; "you can sit here on the other side."

Tode's face flushed a little as he changed his seat, but now another of the boys, having a grudge against Dick, cried out,

"Hunt stuck a pin in him first; I seen him do it."

"You hush up!" muttered Dick, with a scowl.

Just then the superintendent's bell sounded and the lesson time was over.

When the school was dismissed, Mr. Scott detained Tode.

"Why didn't you tell me that Dick had stuck a pin into you first," the teacher asked, rapidly turning the leaves of his Bible as he spoke.

"I ain't a sneak like he is," answered Tode, briefly.

Mr. Scott found the place that he wanted, and keeping his finger between the leaves, looked thoughtfully at the boy before him.

"You told me that your name is Tode. That is what the boys call you. It isn't your real name, is it?" he asked, with a friendly look.

Tode puckered his forehead into a puzzled frown at the question.

"N-no," he answered, slowly. "There's some more to it, but I can't think what 'tis. Wish't I could."

"You've no father or mother?"

"No--never had none since I's big enough to know anything," was the careless reply.

Mr. Scott laid his hand kindly on the lad's shoulder.

"My boy," he said, slowly and earnestly, "I believe yours is a very beautiful name. It must be Theodore."

"That's it! That's it!" exclaimed Tode, excitedly. "I 'member somebody told it to me once, an' I know that's it. How'd you know it so quick?" He looked up wonderingly into his teacher's face as he asked the question.

"I once knew another Theodore who was nicknamed Tode; but, my boy, do you know what your name means?"

Tode shook his head. "Didn't know names meant anything," he answered.

"But they do. Theodore means the gift of God. A boy with such a name as that ought to count for something in the world."

"I mean to." The boy uttered the words slowly and emphatically.

Mr. Scott's face brightened. "Do you mean that you love and serve the Lord Jesus, Theodore?" he asked, softly.

The boy shook his head half sadly, half perplexedly.

"I don't know nothin' much 'bout Him," he answered, with a gentleness most strange and unusual in him, "but I've promised to do the right thing every time now--an' I'm a-goin' to do it."

"You have promised--whom, Theodore?"

84

"Promised myself--but I don't know nothin' much 'bout what is the right thing," he added, in a discouraged tone.

"You'll soon learn if you're in earnest, my boy. This Book will tell you all you need to know. Can you read?"

"Some."

"Then read this verse for me, will you?" Mr. Scott held out his Bible and pointed to the verse.

Slowly and stumblingly the boy read, "Dearly beloved, avenge not yourselves," and again,

"Recompense to no man evil for evil."

Seeing that Tode did not understand the meaning of what he had read, Mr. Scott explained the passages to him. The boy listened attentively, then he exclaimed in a tone of dismay,

"But does it mean that a feller can't never strike back?"

"That's what it says."

Tode pondered this unpalatable statement with a clouded face.

"But what ye goin' to do when some other feller cuts up rough with ye?"

"Find some other way to get even with him."

"But I don't see--what other way is there 'cept hittin' him a harder one'n he gives you?"

Mr. Scott opened his Bible again and pointed to the last two verses of the twelfth chapter of Romans.

Tode went home that day with his mind in a tumult. These new ideas did not suit him at all. A "word and a blow," and the blow first had been his method of settling such questions heretofore, and it seemed to him far the better way.

He took a roundabout route home, for he did not want to see Nan until he had thought out this matter to his own satisfaction. To help people poorer or weaker than himself, or to "keep straight" himself, and help others to do likewise--this was one thing. To meekly submit to ill treatment and "take a blow" from a fellow whom he "could whip with his little finger"--this was quite another and, to one of Tode's temperament, a far more distasteful thing.

The boy had reached no conclusion when he finally went home to supper. He was silent and thoughtful all the evening, but it was not until the following day that he spoke of the matter to Nan.

Nan listened in perplexed silence to what he had to say. She had been well taught while her mother lived, but she had never given these subjects any real, deep thought, as Tode was doing now. She began to feel that this rough, untaught street boy was likely to get far ahead of her if he should keep on pondering over questions like this. Even now she could give him but little help.

Seeing this, Tode took up his Testament again, and read on and on until he had finished the book of Matthew, and gained a pretty clear idea of the life and death of Jesus the Christ. There was much, of course, that he did not understand at all. Many of the words and expressions conveyed no meaning to him, but yet he gathered enough to understand, in a measure, what that Life was, and he began dimly to realise why the bishop gave so much of his time and thought to God's poor. The boy pondered these things in his heart, and a new world seemed to open before him.

"Nan," he said at last, "I've found out what my real name is. It's Theodore."

"Theodore," repeated the girl. "Well, I'm glad to know it, for I never did like to call you Tode. How did you find out?"

"Mr. Scott said it to me, and I knew as soon as I heard it that that was it."

"Then I won't ever call you Tode again. I shall call you Theo. I like that."

The boy liked it too. It gave him a strange thrill of pleasure every time he thought of what Mr. Scott had said about the meaning of his name.

VIII. THEO'S SHADOW WORK

The days that followed were very busy ones for both Nan and Theo. The girl spent most of her time over the stove or the moulding board, and the boy, delivering the supplies to many of the families in the two big tenement houses, attending to his stand, and selling evening papers, found the days hardly long enough for all that he wanted to do.

As he went from room to room with Nan's bread and soup and gingerbread, he soon learned much about the different families and found plenty of opportunities to serve as the "bishop's shadow," in these poor homes. Money he had not to give, for every penny that he could possibly spare was laid aside for a special purpose now, but he found countless ways to carry help and sunshine to sad and sore hearts, without money.

One morning he left Nan's room with a basket piled with bread--brown and white--in one hand, and a big tin pail full of boiled hominy in the other. He went first to the top floor, stopping at one door after another, where dirty, frowzy women and children opened at the sound of his cheery whistle. He handed in the loaves, or the measures of hominy with a gay word or a joke that more than once banished a frown from a woman's worn face, or checked the tears of a tired, hungry child. Children were getting to be fond of the boy now, and he liked it.

In one room there were two families and half a dozen children. In one corner, on a rickety couch was a crippled boy, who had lain there day after day, through long, weary months. He was listening intently for that whistle outside the door, and when he heard it, his dull eyes brightened, and he called out eagerly,

"Oh, tell him to come in a minute--just a minute!"

The woman who opened the door, said indifferently, "Tommy wants you to come in a minute."

Theo stepped over to the tumbled couch, and smiled down into the wistful eyes of the sick boy.

"Hello, old man!" he said, cheerily. "I've brought you something," and out of his pocket he pulled a golden chrysanthemum that he had picked up in the street the day before, and had kept all night in water. It was not very fresh now, but Tommy snatched it hungrily, and gazed at it with a happy smile.

"Oh, how pretty--how pretty it is!" he cried, softly smoothing the golden petals with his little bony forefinger. "Can I keep it, truly?"

"'Course. I brought it for you," Theo answered, his round, freckled face reflecting the boy's delight. "But I must scoot. Folks'll be rowin' me if their bread's late."

He ran off leaving the sick boy with the flower held lovingly against his thin white cheek, while his eyes followed wistfully Theo's strong, active figure as he hurried away.

On the next floor, an old woman, bent and stiffened by rheumatism, sat alone all day, while her children were away at work. She could not get out of her chair, or help herself in any way. Her breakfast would be a penny's worth of Nan's hominy, but on this morning her children had gone off without even setting out a dish, or a cup of water for her.

Tode brought her a saucer and spoon, filled a cup with fresh water from the faucet, and pulled up the curtain so that the sunlight would shine in upon her.

"There, old lady," he said, brightly, when this was done, "now you're all right, an' I'll be in again an' fix your dinner for ye."

The old woman's dim eyes looked after him, and she muttered a word of thanks as she turned slowly to her breakfast.

The boy wasted no minutes, for he had none to spare, but even when he did not step inside a door at all, he always had a smile or a bright word ready for each customer, and in lives where sin or grinding poverty has destroyed all hope, and life has become simply dull, dogged endurance of suffering, a cheerful word or smile has a wonderful power. These wretched women and forlorn little children had already begun to look forward to the coming of the "bread boy," as the little ones called him, as a bright spot in their days. In almost every room he managed to leave a hint of cheer behind him, or at least to lighten a little the cloudy atmosphere.

His pail and basket empty, he ran back to Nan's room for his own supplies, and having opened his stand he served his customers, taking his own breakfast between whiles, as he had opportunity. He sold the morning papers, too, at his stand, and between twelve and one o'clock he was as busy as a boy could well be. After that hour few customers appeared, and then, having made his midday meal from whatever he had left, he closed his stand and went home.

Then was his time for a little more of what Nan called his "shadow work," when he refilled with fresh water the cup of the rheumatic old woman, or carried her a cup of tea that Nan had made for her, adding to it, perhaps, a cooky or a sandwich that remained from his stock. Or he glanced into a room where two or three children were locked in all day while the mothers were away at work--and attended to the fire for them. Often he found time for a five minutes' chat with crippled Tommy, and now and then he walked awhile with a sick baby in his arms as he had seen the bishop do that day long before. They were all little things that the boy did, but as he kept on doing them day after day, he found in this service for others such happiness as he never had known before.

Tommy's delight in the half-withered chrysanthemum set Theo to thinking, and the result of his thinking was that he began to frequent the flower stalls and pick up the broken blossoms that were occasionally thrown aside there.

One day a woman who was selling flowers, said to him, "Say, boy, what do you do with the flowers you pick up? I've seen you 'round here after 'em lots o' times lately."

"Give 'em to sick folks an' poor ones that can't get out anywheres," replied the boy, promptly.

The woman searched his face to see if he were deceiving her, but there was nothing sly or underhanded in the clear eyes that returned her gaze so frankly.

"Hm-m," she murmured, thoughtfully. "What do you do Saturday nights, boy?"

"Nothin' much, after I've sold out my papers."

"Well, Saturday night's our busy time here; one of our busy times, that is, an' if you want to come 'round an' help for an hour or two, I'll pay you in the flowers that are left over."

Theo's eyes brightened, but he was shrewd, and was not going to bind himself to an agreement that might not be satisfactory.

"I'll come next Sat'day an' try it," he said.

"All right," and the woman turned to a customer.

Theo was on hand promptly the next Saturday evening. He found that the flower woman wanted him to carry home pots of growing plants for lady purchasers. He was kept busy until nine o'clock, and received in payment a good-sized basket full of violets, roses, heliotrope and carnations. Some had short stems, and some were a little wilted, but the boy was well content with his pay.

"Most of them will freshen up and look bright as ever if you put them to-night in a pail of water where they'll have plenty of room," the woman said; "and here--this is for good luck," and she handed him a little pot of geranium with a cluster of pink blossoms.

That brought a smile of genuine delight to the boy's face.

"Oh!" he cried, "that's dandy! I'll give it to Nan."

"And who's Nan--your sister?" questioned the woman.

"N--no, not quite. Guess she's as good's my sister, though. Shall I come next Sat'day, ma'am?" replied the boy.

"Yes, come next Saturday, an' right along, if you keep on doing as well's you've done to-night."

Theo almost ran home, so eager was he to show Nan his treasures. He had never cared very much for flowers himself, but he was beginning now to realise their value to others, and he was sure that Nan would be delighted with the geranium.

He was not disappointed. The girl's eyes sparkled at sight of the delicate pink blossoms and she thanked him so heartily that he could only mutter, "Oh, shucks! 'Tain't nothin' much."

Then he showed her his basket of cut flowers, and she exclaimed delightedly over them as she lifted them out as tenderly as if they had been alive, and placed them carefully in a pail of fresh water in which she had sprinkled a little salt.

"Mother used to put salt in the water to keep flowers fresh," she said, "and oh, won't it be lovely to carry these around to the shut-ins, tomorrow, Theo! I think Mrs. Hunt would like some," she added.

"All right. Pick out what you like an' take 'em in to her now."

Nan selected some of the freshest blossoms and went across with them to her neighbour, leaving Theo with the baby, who was asleep. She was gone some time, and when she returned her face was grave.

"What's the matter? Didn't she like 'em?" asked the boy.

"Yes, indeed, she was ever so pleased with them, and told me to thank you for sending them to her--but, Theo, she's worrying so over Dick. She thinks he's going all wrong."

"So he is," answered Theo, soberly.

"And can't you do anything about it?"

"Don't see's I can. He's in with a mean lot o' fellers, 'n he's no good anyhow, nowadays."

"But there must be some good in him. His father and mother are so good," pleaded Nan.

"Mrs. Hunt was crying when I went in. She says Dick often stays out till midnight or after now, and she's afraid he'll be locked up."

"Serve him right if he was," muttered Theo, under his breath.

"He's lost the place his father got for him," added Nan.

"'Course. Nobody'd keep such a feller long."

Nan shook her head sorrowfully, thinking of Dick's mother. Theo said no more, and soon left the room. Nan thought he had gone to bed, but instead, he went out and walked slowly and somewhat doubtfully toward a saloon which he had seen Dick enter more than once of late. Theo, himself, used to go there, but he had not been near the place for many a week. He did not want to go in now, and he waited about outside, wishing that Dick would come out, and yet uncertain what to do if he did come. Finally he pushed open the door and went up the stairs. A dozen or so boys were there, many of whom he knew, and among them was Dick. The proprietor of the place gave the boy a warm welcome, and some of the boys greeted him gaily, but Dick scowled as Theo sat down beside him.

He waited until the loud talk began again, then he said in a low tone, "Dick, I came after you. Will you go home with me now? Your mother's frettin'."

Dick's face darkened angrily.

"Who made you boss over me?" he shouted, springing from his seat with a threatening gesture. "You mind your own business, will you?"

Theo's cheeks flushed as every face in the room was turned toward him.

"What's the row?"

"What's he doin'?"

"What does he want?"

"Put him out! Put him out!"

These shouts and others mingled with oaths as all crowded about the two boys.

"There's no row, an' nothin' to get mad about," said Theo, trying to speak quietly. "Dick's mother's frettin', an' I asked him to go home with me. That's all there is about it."

"An' enough it is too," exclaimed one of the boys. "Dick's big enough to know when to go home, ain't he?"

"What's he got to do with me or my mother?" growled Dick, "I'll go home when I get good an' ready, an' not before."

"An' it's time for you to go home now!" exclaimed the proprietor of the place, elbowing his way to the front of the group, and addressing Theo. "We don't want none o' your sort around here. Now clear out--d'ye hear?"

Seeing that it was useless to stay longer, Theo departed, followed by taunting cries and yells, from all in the room.

He went gloomily homeward, telling himself that he had been a fool to try to do anything for Dick Hunt. Dick was "no good anyhow." But, as he passed her door, Mrs. Hunt opened it and peered anxiously out. Her eyes were red and swollen, and she turned back with a disappointed air as she saw Theo. The next moment however, she stepped out into the hall, pushing the door to behind her.

"Tode," she whispered, "do you know where my Dick is?"

The boy answered reluctantly, "He's down at Todd's."

Mrs. Hunt put her apron to her eyes and sobbed softly. "Oh, dear," she moaned, "his father's gone to look for him, an' if he finds him there he'll most kill him--he's that mad with the boy for the way he's been goin' on lately."

Theo stood silent, not knowing what to say, and then Mrs. Hunt turned back into the room while he went up another flight to his. He had just reached his own door when he heard loud, angry voices accompanied by scuffling sounds on the stairs below, and he knew that Mr. Hunt had found Dick, and was bringing him home.

After Theodore had gone out, Nan had put all the flowers into two big dishes with plenty of water, and the next morning she was up early and separated them, putting together two or three pinks or a rose with its buds and a bit of foliage, or a cluster of geranium blossoms and green leaves.

When Theo came for them she laid the small clusters carefully in a basket, and sprinkled them with fresh water, then as she stooped and buried her face among the fragrant, beautiful things she exclaimed,

"Oh Theo, I wish I had time to go with you, and see how happy you make them all with these beautiful, lovely flowers."

"I'll begin with you," laughed the boy. "Pick out the ones you like best."

But Nan put her hands resolutely behind her and shook her head.

"No, I'm not sick and I've had the pleasure of seeing them all, and fixing them, beside my pot of geranium. That's plenty for me."

Theodore looked critically at her, then at the blossoms; then he picked out three delicate pink carnations.

"No, no! Please don't, Theo," began the girl, but with a laughing glance at her, Theodore laid the blossoms in Little Brother's small white fingers, and hurried away.

He went first to Tommy O'Brien's room. The sick boy's weary face brightened at sight of him, but it fairly beamed when Theodore held up the basket saying, "Choose any one of 'em Tommy--the very prettiest of all."

"O-oh!" cried Tommy. "I never saw so many. Oh, Theo, where did you get 'em all?"

Theo told him while the woman and the children crowded about the basket to see and exclaim over the contents.

Tommy chose a spray of lily of the valley and Theo added a pink rose and bud. Then he gave a blossom to each of the children and to their mothers as well, and went away leaving softened faces and smiles in place of frowns and sullen words.

The old woman whose breakfast was so often forgotten was not alone to-day. Her daughters were at home, but they were not paying much attention to her. At first she peered stupidly with her half-blind eyes into Theo's basket, then suddenly she cried out,

"Oh, I smell 'em! I smell vi'lets. Where be they? Where be they?"

There was one little bunch of violets in the basket. Theo snatched it up and laid it in the wrinkled, trembling hands. The old woman held the blossoms against her withered cheek, then she pressed them to her lips, and two big tears rolled slowly down her face.

"La! Ma's cryin' over them vi'lets. Here Tode, gi' me some o' them bright ones. Gi' me a rose!" cried one of the young women, and Theo handed each of them a rose and went away in silence. He glanced back as he left the room. The old woman was still holding the violets to her cheek and it was plain, even to the boy, that her thoughts were far away.

So, from room to room he went and nowhere did he fail of a glad welcome, because of the gifts he offered. In the dirtiest rooms, the most hardened of the women, the roughest and rudest of the children, seemed to become momentarily gentle and tender when the flowers were laid in their hands.

When all had been given away except one rose, Theodore paused and considered. There were several rooms that he had not visited. To which of these should he carry this last rose?

Not to Old Man Schneider surely. He was standing at the moment outside Old Man Schneider's door. The old man was the terror of all the children in the house, so ugly and profane was he, and so hideous to look at. Fearless as Theodore was--the sight of Old Man Schneider always made him shudder, and the boy had never yet spoken to him.

While he stood there trying to decide who should have the rose, he heard a deep, hollow groan, and surely it came from the room of Old Man Schneider. Theodore stood still and listened. There came another groan and another, and then he knocked on the door. There was no response and he opened it and went in. He had been in many dirty, dismal rooms, but never in one so dirty and so dismal as this. It looked as if it never had been clean. The only furniture was a tumble-down bed in one corner, a chair and a broken stove. On the bed, the old man was lying, covered with rags. He fixed his sunken eyes on the boy and roughly demanded what he wanted, but even as he spoke he groaned again.

"You are sick--can't I do something for you?" asked the boy.

The old man gazed at him for a moment, then he broke into a torrent of angry words, ending with,

"Get out o' my sight. I hate boys. I hate everybody an' everything."

Theodore stood still. The rose in his hand looked strangely out of place in that squalid room--but--beautifully out of place, for it seemed to shed light and color as well as perfume through the close, unhealthy atmosphere.

"Clear out, I say. Why don't ye go?" The old man tried to shake a threatening fist, but his arm dropped weakly, and in spite of himself he moaned with pain.

"Can't I bring a doctor or somebody to help you?" the boy asked gently.

"Ain't nobody ter help me. Don't I tell ye I hate everybody?" was the fierce reply.

Theodore gazed about him. There seemed nothing that he could do. He hesitated for a moment, then stepped forward and laid the beautiful rose against the dark, knotted fingers on the ragged bed-covering, and then he went away, closing the door behind him. Stopping only to put his basket into his room and lock the door, he hurried off to the dispensary and asked that a doctor be sent to Old Man Schneider as soon as possible. He waited until the doctor was at liberty and then returned with him. There was no response to their knock, and again Theodore opened the door and went in, the doctor following.

The old man did not move or look up even when the doctor spoke to him. He lay as Theo had last seen him only that his fingers were closed tightly over the stem of the rose, and one crimson petal lay on the pillow close to the sunken cheek. The old man was dead--but who could tell what thoughts of other days--of sinless days long past, perhaps--may have been awakened in his heart by that fragrant, beautiful bit of God's handiwork?

As Theodore went quietly up the stairs, he was glad that he had not passed by Old Man Schneider's door.

IX. THEO IN TROUBLE

Theo went regularly now to the mission school on Sunday afternoons, and Mr. Scott had become much interested in him.

One day Mr. Scott pleased Theo immensely by going to the boy's stand and getting his lunch there, and not long after he went one evening to the boy's room. He found the place dark and the door locked, but as he was turning away, Theo came running up the stairs.

"Oh!" he cried out, in a tone of pleased surprise, as he saw his teacher. "Wait a minute an' I'll get a light."

Having lighted his lamp, the boy sat down on the cot, giving the broken stool to his visitor. Mr. Scott's heart was full of sympathy as he glanced around the forlorn little room and remembered that it was all the home that the boy had.

"Theodore," he said, after talking a while, "what do you do evenings?"

"Oh, sometimes I stay in Nan's room, an' sometimes I drop in an' talk to Tommy O'Brien or some of the other sick ones in the house, an' sometimes I go somewheres outside. Saturday nights I help at a flower stand."

"Why don't you go to an evening school? I think that would be the best place for you to spend your evenings," said Mr. Scott.

This was a new idea to the boy. He thought it over in silence.

Mr. Scott went on, "It's not your fault, Theodore, that you have had no schooling, thus far, but now, you can go to an evening school and it will be your fault if you grow up ignorant. You will be able to do far more and better work in the world, with an education, than without one. The more you know yourself the better you can help others, you see."

"Yes," sighed the boy. "I guess that's so, but I 'spect I'll find it tough work learning."

"I'm not so sure of that. It will be rather hard at first, because you're not used to studying; but I think you are bright enough to go ahead pretty fast when you once get a good start. Now who is this girl, that I've heard you mention several times--Nan is her name?"

"Oh, yes, Nan. Come on, I want you to see her an' our baby," replied the boy, eagerly.

Somewhat uncertain as to what kind of a girl this might be, yet anxious to know as much as possible about Theo's associates and surroundings, Mr. Scott followed the boy down the stairs.

"Nan, here's my teacher, Mr. Scott, come to see the baby," Theodore exclaimed, as he unceremoniously pushed open the door and ushered in the visitor.

Mr. Scott was more taken aback than was Nan, at this abrupt introduction. The girl coloured a little, but quietly arose and shook hands with the gentleman, while Theo exclaimed:

"Good! Little Brother ain't asleep yet. This is our baby, Mr. Scott. Ain't he a daisy? Take him."

Now, Mr. Scott was a young man and totally unused to "taking" babies, but the boy had lifted the little one from the bed and was holding him out to his teacher with such a happy face that the young man felt that it would never do to disappoint him. So he received the baby gingerly in both hands and set him on his knee, but he did not know what to say or do to amuse the child, and it was an immense relief to him when Little Brother held out his hands to Theo, and the boy took him again saying,

"Ye don't know him yet, do ye, Little Brother? You will though, by 'n' by," wherein Theo was more of a prophet than he imagined.

Relieved of the child, Mr. Scott turned to Nan and the colour rose in his face as he saw a gleam of amusement in the girl's dark eyes, but Theo's ready tongue filled up the momentary pause, and soon all three were chatting like old friends, and when Mr. Scott took his departure, it was with the conviction that his new scholar was fortunate in having Nan for a friend. At the same time he realised that this great tenement with its mixed community was a most unsuitable place for a girl like Nan, and determined that she should be gotten into better surroundings as soon as it could be accomplished.

His interest in Theodore was deepened by this visit to his room and friends. He felt that there was something unusual in the boy, and determined to keep watch of him and give him any needed help.

It was November now and the night was chilly. As Mr. Scott left the tenement house he buttoned his thick overcoat about him, and shivered as he thought of Theodore's bare cot, with not a pillow or a blanket even.

"Not a single bit of bedding," he said, to himself, "and no fire! That will never do, in weather like this."

The next day he mentioned the case to the aunt with whom he lived, with the result that a couple of pillows and a warm comforter were sent before night to Nan's room, addressed to Theodore Bryan, and for the remainder of the winter the boy at least did not suffer from cold at night.

Theodore grew to like his teacher much as the weeks passed, and often after Sunday-school the two walked home together. Some of the boys that had been longer in the class rather resented this friendship, the more so as Theo was by no means popular among them just at this time.

"He's gettin' too good, Tode Bryan is," one of them said, one Sunday. "He walked home with teacher last week, an' now he's a doin' it again." He glanced gloomily after the two, as he spoke.

"I'd like ter punch his head; that's what I'd like to do," put in another. "He pitched inter me for swearin' t'other day."

"He's a fine one to talk 'bout swearin'," added a third. "I've heard him goin' it hot an' heavy many a time."

"Oh yes, but he's settin' up fer a saint now, ye know," said Dick Hunt, scornfully. "I owe him a lickin,' an' he'll get it too 'fore he's many days older."

"What for, Dicky?" questioned another.

"What for? For blabbin' to my daddy an' sendin' him to Todd's after me, the night he come sneakin' in there himself," cried Dick. "I've been layin' for him ever since, an' I'll give it to him good, first chance I get."

"He goes to night school now," remarked one.

"Oh, yes, he's puttin' on airs all 'round," returned Dick. "I'll night school him!" he added, vengefully.

It was not long before Dick found an opportunity to execute his threats of vengeance. He was loafing on a street corner, with Carrots and two other boys, one night, when Theodore passed them on his way home from school. He nodded to them as he went by, but did not stop. Dick's eyes followed him with a threatening glance until he saw him turn through a narrow street. Then Dick held a brief conference with Carrots and the other two, and all four set off hastily in the direction that Theodore had taken.

He, meantime, went on whistling cheerily and thinking pleasant thoughts, for he was beginning to get on at the school, and better yet, he had in his pocket at that moment, a five-dollar bill that meant a great deal to him.

Ever since his return from the bishop's house, he had been working as he never had worked before, neglecting no opportunity to earn even a nickel, and every penny that he could possibly spare he had given to Nan to keep for him. He had been perfectly frank with her, and she knew that as soon as he had saved up thirty-seven dollars he meant to carry it to the bishop for Mrs. Russell, and tell him the whole story. First, to stop all his wrongdoing and then as far as possible, to make up to those he had wronged--these were Theodore's firm purposes now, but he felt that he could never bear to face the bishop again until he could take with him the proof of his genuine repentance.

Many and many a time in these past weeks, had the boy planned with Nan how he would go to the house and what he would say to the bishop, and what he hoped the bishop would say to him, and Nan had rejoiced almost as much as the boy himself as, week by week, the sum in her hands grew toward the desired amount. Even Nan did not know all the hard work and stern self-denial that had made it possible for Theodore to put by that money out of his small earnings.

The five in his pocket on this evening would complete the entire sum and the very next day he meant to carry it to the bishop. The mere thought of seeing again the face that was to him like no other face in all the world-- filled the boy's heart with a deep, sweet delight. He was thinking of it as he hurried along through a short, dark alley, where were only two or three stables and one empty house.

Quick, stealthy footsteps followed him, but he paid no heed to them until a heavy blow on the back of his head made him suddenly turn and face four dark figures that were close at his heels. "Who are you? What ye hittin' me for?" he demanded, angrily.

There was no response, but Dick struck at him again. This time, however, Theodore was on his guard, and he caught Dick's arm and gave it a twist that made its owner cry out.

"Oh ho, it's you, Dick Hunt. I might a' known nobody else would sneak up on a feller this way. Well, now, what are ye after?"

"I'm after givin' you the worst lickin' ever you had," muttered Dick, trying in vain to free his arm from Theo's strong grip.

"What for?" demanded Theodore.

"For sneakin' into Todd's and then runnin' to tell my father where I was. That's one thing, but there's plenty more't I'm goin' to settle with you for, to-night," shouted Dick, as he pounded with his left hand, and kicked viciously at the other's shins.

"I never spoke to your father that night," Theo declared, but Dick responded, scornfully,

"Tell that to a greenhorn! Pitch into him, boys. He won't let go o' me."

Seeing the others start toward him, Theo flung Dick's arm aside, and bracing himself against a vacant house just behind him, faced them all in dogged silence. They hesitated for a moment, but Dick cried out again,

"Come on, boys!" and the four flung themselves upon Theo, striking, pounding and kicking all together. He defended himself as best he could, but the odds were too great. It was only when the boy slipped to the ground in a limp, motionless heap, that his assailants drew off, and looked uneasily at one another in the darkness.

"What'll we do now?" whispered Carrots.

"Cut it--somebody's comin'!" cried Dick, in a low tone, and thereupon they took to their heels, leaving Theo as he had fallen on the ground.

The boys stopped running as soon as they reached a lighted street where the passers-by might notice them; but they walked on rapidly and discussed the affair in low, guarded tones.

"You don't think he's done for, do ye, Dick?" questioned Carrots, uneasily.

Dick tried to laugh carelessly, but the effort was a failure. He was beginning to be anxious as to the result, though he was not ready to admit it.

"Done for? Not much!" he answered, promptly. "More like he was shammin', an' wasn't hurt half so much as he'd ought ter be."

"But if 'tain't so-if he's hurt bad, he may have us up for 'sault an' batt'ry," remarked another.

"Dick's the only one he could go for, 'cause 'twas so dark, he couldn't spot the rest of us," put in Carrots, hastily.

"Ye needn't try to sneak out o' it that way," cried Dick, sharply. "If I get took up, you'll be, too."

"D'ye mean't you'd give us away after gettin' us into it, jest ter help you out?" demanded the other, in a threatening tone.

"If he does, we'll make it hot fer him" put in another, as Dick answered, doubtfully,

"Wal if he should make a fuss 'bout it, I can't take all the blame, can I? I didn't do all the whackin'."

"Well, I say, boys, he's a nice one, Dick Hunt is! After gettin' us to help him lick a feller 'cause he darsent do it alone, he talks of gettin' us took up for it," exclaimed the last speaker; "but see here, you," he added to Dick, "Bryan knew you an' he didn't know any the rest of us, an' I tell ye what--if you get inter trouble 'bout this job, you lug us into it 'f ye dare! I'll swear 't Carrots an' Jo here were down t' my place with me, 'n' they'll swear to it too; hey, boys?"

"We will so!"

"We'll do that ev'ry time!" they answered in one voice; and then with a few cutting words the three turned off together, leaving Dick to pursue his way alone.

And miserable enough Dick was as he walked on alone. He was not in the least sorry for what had been done to Theodore, but he was afraid of the consequences. He turned sick with dread as he remembered how the boy's body had slipped in a limp heap to the ground and lain there motionless.

Suppose they had killed him? It would be murder. Somebody would have to answer for it and that somebody would be he--Dick Hunt. The cold perspiration started on his forehead and his heart throbbed heavily at the thought, and he felt a wild desire to run on and on till he had left that dark heap in the dark alley, miles and miles behind him.

Then came a flash of hope. Perhaps after all Tode was not so badly hurt. Perhaps he had been shamming just to scare them. At this thought, Dick's quick pace slackened and he had half a mind to go back and see if the body still lay there, but he could not bring himself to do that. He shivered and hurried on aimlessly, through the brightly lighted streets. He was afraid to go home, lest he be met there by the news that he dreaded. He was afraid to stay in the streets, for every moment he expected to feel the heavy hand of a policeman on his shoulder. He said to himself that Carrots and the others might inform against him just to save themselves.

So, as wretched as a boy well could be, he wandered about for an hour or two, stopping sometimes in dark corners and then hastening on again, stealing suspicious glances over his shoulders, and listening for pursuing footsteps. At last, he turned homeward, longing, yet dreading, to see his mother.

It was nearly midnight when he crept softly up the stairs, but his mother had been unable to sleep, and as his hand touched the door in the darkness, she threw it open with a sigh of relief that her weary waiting was over for that night. She did not find fault with him. It seemed to her utterly useless now to complain or entreat.

Dick longed to ask if she knew anything about Tode, but his tongue refused to utter the words and he tumbled into bed in gloomy silence.

There had been no shamming when Theo fell under the brutal blows of the four boys who had set upon him. They were all strong, well-grown lads, and striking blindly and viciously in the dark, had perhaps hit harder than they realised. At any rate Theo had felt his strength failing even before a last blow on his head made him unconscious of what followed.

The "somebody," whom the boys had heard, came slouching along through the dark alley and stumbled over the prostrate body.

"Hello! What's this?" he exclaimed, his nimble fingers running rapidly over the boy's face and figure. "Somebody's been up to something here. Let's see if--no! Well, that's queer!"

These disconnected remarks were the accompaniment to a rapid and skillful search through the boy's pockets, and the last emphatic expression was drawn forth by the discovery that there had been no robbery; whereupon the newcomer promptly proceeded to complete the job by emptying the said pockets in a manner that proved him no novice at such business. Then he stole noiselessly away, leaving the boy again alone in the darkness, and now there was no good bishop at hand to take him in.

Meantime, at home, Nan was wondering why Theo did not come in as usual to tell her what he had been doing at the night school, and to get Tag, who always staid with her when Theo was at the school. Tag was troubled and uneasy too. When it was time for the boy to come Tag sat watching the door, his ears alert for a footstep outside. Now and then he whined, and finally he showed so plainly his desire to go out that Nan opened the door, saying,

"Go find him, Tag."

She stood in her doorway listening, and heard the dog scamper up to Theo's door. There he listened and nosed about for a moment, then down he came again, and with a short, anxious bark, dashed down the stairs to the street. Nan waited a long time but the dog did not return, and at last she put out her light and went to bed with a troubled heart.

But Tag could not sleep. He seemed to know that there was something wrong and something for him to attend to. He raced first to his master's stand, then to the mission school and to the night school, and finding all these places now dark and silent, he pattered through the streets, his nose close to the ground, his anxious, loving eyes watching everything that moved. So at last he came to that dark heap in the dark alley, and first he was wild with joy, but when his frantic delight failed to awaken his master and make him come away home, Tag was sure that something was very wrong indeed and he began to run backward and forward between the motionless body and the corner, until he attracted the attention of a policeman who followed him around into the dark alley, and in a few minutes Theodore was on his way to the Emergency Hospital with Tag following after the ambulance at the top of his speed. But once again Tag found himself rudely repulsed when he tried to slip in after his master. This time he felt that he really could not bear it, and so he stood on the hospital steps and lifting up his voice howled his protest until somebody came and drove him away. But he couldn't stay away, so he crawled into a dark corner up against the wall, and curling himself into the smallest possible space, lay there watchful and wretched until morning, when, after eyeing wistfully those who came out and went in past him, he trotted slowly home to Nan, and did his poor best to tell her what had happened and where Theo was.

Nan had passed an anxious night, for she was sure that there was something wrong, and since Theo's return from the bishop's, he had been so changed, that she had grown very fond of him. Being a year or two his senior, she felt a kind of elder sisterly responsibility in regard to him, knowing as she did, that he was even more alone in the world than she, for she had Little Brother, and Theo had nobody at all.

So she was at Mrs. Hunt's door, talking the matter over with her, when Tag, with drooping head and tail, came slowly up the stairs. He wagged his tail faintly at sight of Nan, and rubbed his head affectionately against her, and then stood looking up at her, as if waiting to be questioned.

"He's been gone all night," Nan was saying to Mrs. Hunt, and referring to the dog, "but I don't believe he found Theo. He doesn't act as if he had. Oh, Mrs. Hunt, where do you suppose he is?"

Mrs. Hunt shook her head. "The dear knows," she said, "but something must 'a' happened to him, sure. He's been steady as clockwork since ever he took that room upstairs, I'll say that for him." She sighed as she spoke, thinking of her Dick.

"But what can I do, Mrs. Hunt?" cried Nan, her eyes full of tears. "It seems dreadful to keep right on, just as if he were here, as usual. Isn't there any way to find out where he is?"

"Look here, Nan," exclaimed Mrs. Hunt.

"Do you know where his teacher--that Mr. Scott--lives?"

"Yes."

"Well, why don't you send word to him? He seems to think a lot of Tode an' Dick. I guess he does of all his scholars. He would know what to do, an' where to look for the boy--don't you think so?"

Nan's face had brightened as her friend spoke.

"I'm sure that's a good idea," she replied. "He's always been so nice and kind to Theo. I most know he'll help find him."

"That's right now, child, stop fretting, for I'll warrant he'll set things straight in no time. I'll let Dick or Jimmy go around to Mr. Scott's as soon as they've had their breakfast."

Relieved by this promise, and trying hard to be hopeful and not to worry, Nan ran back to her room, while Mrs. Hunt called the boys.

Dick pretended to be very sound asleep, and it required more than one call and shake to arouse him, but in reality, he too had passed a most miserable night, and he had listened, with heart beating fast and hard, to his mother's colloquy with Nan; and as he listened, ever before his mind's eye was that dark, motionless heap on the ground. In imagination, he saw Theo's dead body on a slab in the morgue, and himself in a prison cell, condemned for murder. Dick's worst enemy could not have wished him to be any more wretched than he was in that hour, as he cowered in his bed, and strained his ears to catch every word that was uttered. But when his mother shook him, he rubbed his eyes, and pretended to be still half asleep, and flatly refused to go to Mr. Scott's.

"Let Jim go, 'f anybody's got to," he growled, as he began to pull on his clothes. "Here you, Jim, turn out lively now!" he added, yanking the bedclothes off his brother to emphasise his words.

"He's always a-puttin' off on me--Dick is," snarled Jim, as he joined his mother in the other room a few minutes later, but when he learned why he was to go to Mr. Scott's he made no further objections, but swallowed his breakfast hastily, and went off on the run. Jim did not share his brother's enmity toward the missing boy. Jim liked Theo. He liked Nan too, and was always ready to do an errand for her, if she wanted him.

Mr. Scott was just sitting down to breakfast when Jim appeared, and he left his coffee to cool while he listened with keen interest to what the boy had to tell him. His face was very grave as he said,

"Tell Miss Nan that I will be around there within an hour. See here, though, Jim,--have you had your breakfast?"

"Ye--yes, sir," Jim answered, with a quick glance at the hot cakes and chops that had such an appetising odour. Jim didn't have chops and hot cakes for breakfast.

"Aunt Mary, can you put another plate here for Jim?" Mr. Scott asked, and his aunt, with a smile, set another chair at the table, and piled a plate with eatables, of which the boy disposed as easily and speedily as if that had been his first meal that day.

Mr. Scott likewise made a hasty breakfast, and then he sent Jim back to Nan, while he himself went to his place of business to arrange for his absence that morning.

Within the hour, as he had said, he knocked at Nan's door. She welcomed him with a feeling of glad relief, assured that at least he would be able to find out where Theo was. He waited only to get what little information she could give him, and then set forth, but before he had reached the bottom of the first flight of stairs, Nan ran after him.

"Mr. Scott," she called. "Wouldn't it be a good plan to take Tag--Theo's dog--with you?"

Mr. Scott thought it would, but now an unexpected obstacle was encountered. Tag refused to go with him. He crept under Nan's dress, and crouched there, looking quietly out at the gentleman, but making no movement toward him, though he called and whistled as persuasively as he could.

"Oh, Tag, do go," pleaded Nan, almost ready to cry at the dog's unexpected obstinacy.

Tag twisted his head and looked up at her, and it almost seemed as if he were moved by her pleading tone, for, after a moment's hesitation, he crept slowly out from his refuge, and followed Mr. Scott down the stairs. Once outside the house he stopped and gazed with keen, questioning eyes at the gentleman, standing, meanwhile, ready to dart off, should any attempt be made to capture him, but Mr. Scott stopped too, and said quietly,

"Go find him, Tag. Find Theo."

That was enough for the intelligent little creature. With a quick, sharp yelp of satisfaction, Tag set off at such a pace that Mr. Scott had hard work to keep him in sight. In fact, as soon as they turned into a thronged business street, he lost sight of his four-footed guide entirely, but the direction Tag had taken was a sufficient clue. The young man was so certain that the Emergency Hospital was the place to which the dog was leading him, that he boarded a car and went directly there, and sure enough on the steps sat Tag, his short ears erect, and his eager eyes watching impatiently for a chance to slip inside the doors.

He seemed to know that his chance had come when he saw Mr. Scott running up the steps, for he frisked about and showed his delight in every conceivable fashion. Dogs were not allowed in the hospital, but when Mr. Scott picked Tag up in his arms and promised to keep him there, the attendant finally consented that he should do so. And so they went first to the waiting-room and then up the stairs and through the long corridors.

X. A BITTER DISAPPOINTMENT

Theodore was still unconscious when he was lifted into the ambulance the night before, but on the way to the hospital he opened his eyes, wondering much to find himself flat on his back and being driven rapidly through the streets. In a few minutes he remembered what had happened, and guessed that he must have been stunned by a blow or a fall. As he reached this conclusion, the vehicle stopped, and he was lifted out and carried into the hospital in spite of his protests. He had a dread of entering a hospital as a patient, and he wanted to go home.

But the doctors would not allow him to go home. They told him that if he would be quiet and do as they said, he would probably be able to go home the next morning, and with this promise he was obliged to be content, and allow himself to be undressed and put to bed. He was badly bruised and his right shoulder was very lame, but there was no serious injury, and it seemed to the boy very trying to be compelled to spend the night where he was. He did not sleep much, partly because of his strange surroundings, and partly because of his aching head and shoulder, and as he lay there in the dimly-lighted ward, his thoughts were busy.

A hot anger burned in his heart as he recalled the cowardly attack in the dark alley. He saw that it had been deliberately planned by Dick Hunt, and that the four boys must have followed him from the corner where he saw them.

"I'll pay that Dick Hunt for this," he muttered under his breath, "an' Carrots, too. I know the chap that hit so hard was Carrots. I'll make 'em suffer for it!"

He lay there, his eyes flashing and his cheeks burning, as he thought over various schemes of vengeance. Then suddenly he thought of Mr. Scott, and that brought something else to his remembrance. He seemed to see his teacher holding out his little Bible and making him--Theodore--read aloud those two verses:

"Dearly beloved avenge not yourselves."

And "Recompense to no man evil for evil."

As he repeated these words to himself, the fire died slowly out of the boy's eyes and the angry colour faded from his cheeks. He turned restlessly in his bed and tried to banish these thoughts and bring back his schemes of vengeance, but he could not do it. He knew what was the right--what he ought to do--but he was not willing to do it. Hour after hour he argued the matter with himself, finding all sorts of reasons why, in this case, he might take vengeance into his own hands and "learn that Dick Hunt a lesson," yet feeling and knowing in the depths of his heart that whatever the old Tode Bryan might have done, Theodore Bryan, who was trying to be the bishop's shadow, certainly had no right to do evil to somebody else simply because that somebody had done evil to him.

It was nearly morning before the long battle with himself was over, but it ended at last, and it was Theodore, and not Tode who was victorious, and it was the memory of the bishop's face, and of the bishop's prayer that day in the poorhouse, that finally settled the matter.

"He'd fight for somebody else, the bishop would, but he wouldn't ever fight for himself, an' I mustn't neither," the boy murmured, softly, and then with a long breath he turned his face to the wall and fell asleep, and he had but just awakened from that sleep when Mr. Scott, with Tag under his arm, came through the long corridor to the ward where Theodore was lying in the very last cot, next the wall.

Mr. Scott had promised not to let the dog out of his arms, but if he had been better acquainted with Tag he would never have made such a rash promise. As the gentleman followed the nurse into the ward, the dog's eyes flashed a swift glance over the long line of cots, and the next instant something dark went flying down the room and up on to that last cot in the row, and there was Tag licking his master's face and hands, and wagging his tail, and barking like mad.

"Dear me!" exclaimed the nurse, running toward the corner. "This will never do. He'll drive the patients into fits! Why didn't you keep hold of him?"

She threw the question back in a reproachful tone to Mr. Scott.

He laughed a little as he answered, "If you will try to pick him up now and hold him, you will understand why."

Even as he spoke, the nurse was making an attempt to capture and silence the noisy little fellow. She might as well have tried to pick up a ball of quicksilver. Tag slipped through her fingers like an eel, scurrying from one end of the cot to the other, and barking excitedly all the time.

"Can't you stop him, Theodore?" exclaimed Mr. Scott, as he reached the corner where the boy lay.

"Here, Tag, lie down and be still," cried the boy, and with one last defiant yap at the nurse, Tag nosed aside the bedclothes and snuggled down beside his master with a sigh of glad content.

"Well, if ever I let a dog into my ward again!" exclaimed the nurse, in a tone of stern determination.

"I'm sorry he made such a noise, ma'am. It was only because he was so glad to find me," said Theodore, quickly.

The nurse turned away in offended silence, and Mr. Scott sat down by the bed and began to talk with the boy.

He listened with a grave face to Theo's story. When it was ended, he asked, "Did you recognise either of the boys?"

"Yes, sir; one, certainly, and I think I know one of the others."

"Well?" said the teacher, inquiringly.

Theodore hesitated a moment, then answered in a low tone, "You 'member them verses you showed me that first Sunday, Mr. Scott?"

The gentleman smiled down into the sober, boyish face. "I remember," he replied, "but, Theo, this is a grave matter. To beat a boy until he is unconscious, and then leave him to live or die, is a crime. Such boys ought not to be shielded."

"Mr. Scott, I had an awful time over that last night," answered the boy, earnestly. "I wanted to pay them fellers for this job--you better b'lieve I did, but," he shook his head slowly, "I can't do it. You see, sir, I ain't Tode no more--I'm Theodore, now."

There was a look on the homely, boyish face that forbade further discussion of the matter, and, after a moment's silence, Mr. Scott said in a different tone, "Well, my boy, when are you going home? Nan and the baby want to see you."

Theo glanced impatiently about the long room.

"She said I'd got to stay in bed till the doctor had seen me," he replied, "'n the doctor'll be here 'bout nine o'clock."

"She" was the nurse.

"It's nearly nine now. I'll wait until the doctor comes, then," Mr. Scott said.

The doctor pronounced the boy quite fit to leave the hospital, and his clothes being brought to him, the curtains were drawn around his cot and he dressed himself hastily. But as he pushed aside the curtains, Mr. Scott saw a troubled look on his face, and asked:

"What's the matter, Theodore?"

Without answering the boy crossed the room to the nurse.

"Where's the money that was in my pocket?" he asked, anxiously.

The nurse looked at him sharply. "If there was any money in your pockets when you were brought here it would be in them now," she answered, shortly. "You can go to the office and ask any questions you like."

Theodore turned toward his teacher a very sorrowful face.

114

"I've been robbed, too," he said.

"Oh, I'm sorry, Theodore. How much have you lost?"

"Five dollars. She says to ask at the office, but 'twon't do no good, I s'pose."

"No, nothing would have been taken from your pockets here, but we will stop at the office and see if we can learn anything," Mr. Scott said.

Tag had kept close to his master's heels, and now at his teacher's suggestion Theodore picked up the dog, who went forth quietly enough in that fashion.

Inquiries at the office convinced the boy that he had been robbed before he was brought there, and naturally enough he came to the conclusion that his money had gone into the pockets of Dick Hunt and his companions.

At the door of the tenement house Mr. Scott left Theo, who hurried eagerly up the stairs. On the landing he met Jimmy Hunt, who called out:

"Hi--o, Tode, where ye been all night? Say, what was the matter? Did Mr. Scott find ye?"

"Yes," was Theo's only response, as he pushed open Nan's door, to be greeted with such a warm welcome that he hardly knew what to say and had to hide his embarrassment by poking the baby's ribs to make him laugh. Jimmy Hunt had followed him into the room and listened with open mouth as well as ears to the brief story that the boy told in reply to Nan's questions.

"Oh, 'twasn't much. I got knocked down an' carried to the hospital, an' they wouldn't let me come away till morning--that's all."

"An' wasn't ye hurt?" cried Jimmy, in a disappointed tone. It seemed to him altogether too tame an affair if nobody was hurt.

"My shoulder's sprained, an' my head was hurt a little," Theo answered. "Say, Jim, where's Dick?"

"I d'know. Out somewheres," replied Dick's brother, indifferently.

115

"Why ain't you in school, Jimmy?" was Theo's next question.

"Well, I like that!" exclaimed Jimmy, in a tone of deep disgust. "Ain't I been a-racin' all over town for you this mornin', a-gettin' Mr. Scott to hunt ye up, an' goin' ter see 'f your stand's open, an' carryin' things 'round fer Nan, too? How could I do all that an' be in school, I'd like to know?"

"'Deed, you couldn't, Jimmy," replied Nan, soothingly. "I don't know what I should have done this morning without him, Theo. He was my right hand man."

Jimmy coloured with satisfaction at this high praise, and his delight was complete when Theodore added,

"That so? Well now, Jimmy boy, I ain't goin' to forget this."

"Huh! Twarn't nothin'. I liked to do it," replied Jimmy, and then overcome by a sudden and unaccountable fit of bashfulness he ran hastily out of the room.

Then Theodore told Nan the details of his adventure, but not even to her would he tell the name of his enemy, and Nan did not guess, for she would never have imagined that Mrs. Hunt's Dick could have served Theo so.

Dick had gone out as usual after breakfast and did not come home even to get his supper, but of late his habits had been so irregular that nothing was said at home about his absence.

After supper Jimmy was sent out on an errand and Dick met him and questioned him in regard to Theo's return, and what he had to say. Jimmy waxed indignant over the story which he filled in from his own imagination with many vivid details.

"Some fellers pitched into him an' knocked him down an' beat him an' left him for dead an' they took him t' the hospital an' kep' him there all night. Guess them fellers'll suffer for it! They robbed him, too. Took five dollars out o' his pockets."

116

"They didn't neither!" exclaimed Dick, hastily, thrown off his guard by this unexpected statement.

"Come now, Dick Hunt, mebbe you know more'n I do about it," retorted Jimmy, with withering sarcasm, little suspecting how much more his brother did know. "Mebbe you heard what Nan said to ma 'bout it."

"No, no! 'Course I d'know nothin' 'bout it. How would I know?" replied Dick, quickly and uneasily. "Say, Jimmy, is he--is Tode goin' to have them fellers took up?"

"'Spect he is--I would," answered Jimmy; then remembering his errand, he ran off, leaving Dick looking after him with a haggard, miserable face.

"Robbed," Dick said to himself, as he walked moodily and aimlessly on. "We didn't do that anyhow. Somebody must 'a' gone through his pockets after we cleared out. Nice box I'm in now!"

Dick did not go home at all that night. He was afraid that he might be arrested if he did.

"He knows 'twas me did it, an' he's keepin' dark 'bout it till they can nab me," he thought.

He hunted up the three boys who had been so ready to help him the night before, but he found them now firmly banded together against him. Moreover, they had spread such reports of him among their companions, that Dick found himself shunned by them all. He dared not go home, so he wandered about the streets, eating in out-of-the-way places, and sleeping where he could. One day Carrots told him that Tode Bryan was huntin' everywhere for him. Then Dick, in desperation, made up his mind to go to sea--he could stand the strain no longer. He dared not go home, even to bid his mother goodbye. Dick was selfish and cruel, but he had even yet a little lingering tenderness for his mother. It was not enough to make him behave himself and do what he knew would please her, but it did make him wish that he could see her just for a moment before going away. It was enough to make him creep cautiously to the house after dark, and stand in the

117

shadow, looking up at her window, while he pictured to himself the neat, pleasant room, where at that hour, she would be preparing supper. While he stood there, Theo came out of the house, with Tag, as usual, at his heels. Tag ran over to the dark corner and investigated Dick, but cautiously, for there was no friendship between him and this member of the Hunt family. Dick stood silent and motionless afraid that the dog might bark and draw Theo over there, but he stood ready for flight until Theo whistled and Tag ran back to him, and presently followed him off in another direction. Then, with a breath of relief, Dick stole off into the darkness, and the next day he left the city on a vessel bound for South America, rejoicing that at last he was beyond reach of Tode Bryan.

Dick was not mistaken in thinking that Theo had been searching for him, but he was greatly mistaken as to the boy's purpose in it. Theodore was entirely ready now to obey that command that Mr. Scott had shown him and to do his best to "overcome evil with good." He took it for granted that Dick and the others had robbed as well as beaten him, but all the same, he felt that he was bound to forget all that and find some way to show them a kindness. But though Theo was always on the lookout for him, Dick managed to keep out of his sight while he remained in the city. After Dick had sailed, some boy told Jimmy where his brother had gone, and so at last the news reached Theodore.

Since his return from the bishop's, Theo had had few idle moments, but after losing the five dollars he worked early and late to make up the loss. He grew more silent and thoughtful, and when alone his thoughts dwelt almost continually on that happy day when he should look once more into the bishop's kind face.

"I'll tell him all about it," he would say to himself, "how I saw that Mrs. Russell drop the pocketbook, an' how I slipped under the wagon an' snatched it up out o' the mud, an' used the money. I'll tell it all, an' ev'rything else bad that I can 'member, so he'll know jest what a bad lot I've been, an' then I'll tell him how sorry I am, an' how I'm a-huntin' ev'rywhere for that Jack Finney, an' how I'll keep a-huntin' till I find him."

All this and much more Theodore planned to tell the bishop, and, as he thought about it, it seemed as if he could not wait another hour, so intense was his longing to look once more into that face that was like no other earthly face to him, to listen again to the voice that thrilled his heart, and hear it say, "My boy, I forgive you." Many a time he dreamt of this and started up from sleep with those words ringing in his ears, "My boy, I forgive you," and then finding himself alone in his dark, dismal little room, he would bury his wet cheeks in the pillow and try to stifle the longing in his lonely, boyish heart.

Even Nan, who knew him better than did any one else, never guessed how his heart hungered to hear those words from the lips of the bishop.

But little by little--in nickels and dimes and quarters--Theodore laid by another five dollars. He knew to a penny how much there was, but when he brought the last dime, he and Nan counted it all to make sure. There was no mistake. It amounted to thirty-seven dollars and twenty-five cents, and the boy drew a long, glad breath as he looked up at Nan with shining eyes and flushed cheeks, saying,

"To-morrow, Nan, I can see--him!"

"Don't look so--so awfully glad, Theo. I'm afraid something will happen," said Nan, with a troubled expression in her eyes as she looked at him.

"Don't you worry. I ain't a-goin' to be robbed again--you better believe I ain't!" cried the boy. Then he glanced at his worn suit and tried to pull down his jacket sleeves, as he added, wistfully, "D'you think I look well enough to go there, Nan? I wanted to buy a collar an' necktie, but, I just couldn't wait any longer."

Nan's private opinion was, that if the bishop could only see Theo's face at that moment, the garments he wore would be a matter of small importance. She answered, quickly,

"You look plenty well enough, Theo. Don't worry about that."

She gathered up the money and put it back into the box in which it had been kept, and the boy went across the room to the bed where the baby lay asleep.

"Seems to me he looks kind o' peaked--don't he, Nan?" he remarked, uneasily.

Nan cast an anxious glance at the little, thin face, and shook her head. "He doesn't get strong as I hoped he would," she answered, sadly.

"Oh well, he will, when it comes warmer, so he can get out doors oftener," the boy said, as he went away to his room.

He hurried through his work the next day, closing his stand at the earliest possible moment, and rushing home to get ready for his visit. He always, now, kept his face and hands scrupulously clean. His hair might have been in better condition if he had had money to buy a comb or a brush, but those were among the luxuries that he felt he must deny himself until he had made all the restitution in his power.

To-day, however, when he went to Nan's room for his money, she offered him the use of her comb, and helped him reduce his rough, thick hair to some kind of order. Even then he looked at himself somewhat doubtfully. His suit was so shabby in spite of Nan's careful mending, and his shoes were worse than his suit, but they were polished to the last degree. He had exchanged a sandwich and two doughnuts for that "shine."

"You look well enough, Theo," Nan said, "plenty well enough. Now go on, and oh, I do hope it will be all right."

"I know 'twill," cried the boy, joyously, as he tucked the money carefully into an inside pocket. "Oh, Nan!"

He looked at her with such a happy face that her own beamed a bright response. Then he ran off and Nan stood in the doorway watching him as he went down the stairs, closely followed by his inseparable companion, Tag.

"The dear boy! He is fairly pale," said Nan, to herself, as she turned back into her room. "It is strange how he loves that bishop--and what a different boy he is, too, since he came home. I don't see how the bishop can help loving him. Oh, I do hope nothing will happen to spoil his visit. He has looked forward to it so long."

The boy felt as if he were walking on air as he went rapidly through the crowded streets, seeing nothing about him, so completely were his thoughts occupied with the happiness before him. As he got farther up town the crowd lessened, and when he turned into the street on which the bishop lived, the passers-by were few.

At last he could see the house. In a few minutes he would reach it. Then his joyous anticipations suddenly vanished and he began to be troubled.

What if Brown wouldn't let him in, he thought, or--what if the bishop should refuse to see him or to listen to his story?

As these thoughts came to him his eager pace slackened and for a moment he was tempted to turn back. Only for a moment, however. He knew that the bishop would not refuse to see him, and as for Brown, if Brown refused to admit him, he would go to the servants' door and ask for Mrs. Martin.

So thinking, he pushed open the iron gate and went slowly up the walk.

"Stay here, Tag. Lie down, sir!" he ordered, and the dog obediently dropped down on the steps, keeping his bright eyes fastened on his master, as the boy rang the bell. Theo could almost hear his heart beat as he waited. Suddenly the door swung open and there was Brown gazing severely at him.

"Well--what do you want?" questioned the man, brusquely.

"I want--Don't you know me, Brown? I want to see--Mrs. Martin."

The boy's voice was thick and husky, and somehow he could not utter the bishop's name to Brown standing there with that cold frown on his face.

"Oh--you want to see Mrs. Martin, do you? Well, I think you've got cheek to come here at all after leaving the way you did," Brown growled. He held the door so that the boy could not enter, and seemed more than half inclined to shut it in his face.

"Oh, please, Brown, do let me in," pleaded the boy, with such a heart-broken tone in his voice, that Brown relented--he wasn't half so gruff as he pretended to be--and answered, grudgingly,

"Well, come in, if you must, an' I'll find out if Mrs. Martin will see you."

With a sudden gleam of joy in his eyes, Theodore slipped in.

"Come along!" Brown called over his shoulder, and the boy followed to the housekeeper's sitting-room. The door of the room stood open, and Mrs. Martin sat by the window with a newspaper in her hand. She glanced up over her spectacles as Brown's tall figure appeared at the door.

"Mrs. Martin, this boy says he wants to see you," he announced, and then sauntered indifferently away to his own quarters.

Mrs. Martin took off her glasses as she called, "Come in, boy, and tell me what you want."

Theo walked slowly toward her hoping that she would recognise him, but she did not. Indeed it was a wonder that Brown had recognised him, so different was his appearance in his rough worn clothes, from that of the handsomely dressed lad, whose sudden departure had so grieved the kindhearted housekeeper.

"Don't you know me, Mrs. Martin?" the boy faltered, sorrowfully, as he paused beside her chair.

"No, I'm sure I--why! You don't mean to say that you are our deaf and dumb boy!" exclaimed the good woman, as she peered earnestly into the grey eyes looking down so wistfully into hers.

"Yes, I'm the bad boy you were so good to, but I've been keepin' straight ever since I was here, Mrs. Martin," he answered, earnestly. "I have, truly."

"Bless your dear heart, child," cried the good woman, springing up hastily and seizing the boy's hands. "I'm sure you have. I guess I know a bad face when I see one, and it don't look like yours. Sit down, dear, and tell me all about it."

In the fewest possible words Theo told his story, making no attempt to excuse anything. The housekeeper listened with keen interest, asking a question now and then, and reading in his face the confirmation of all he said. He did not say very much about the bishop, but the few words that he did say and the look in his eyes as he said them, showed her what a hold upon the boy's heart her master had so unconsciously gained, and her own interest in the friendless lad grew deeper.

When his story was told, she wiped her eyes as she said, slowly, "And to think that you've been working all these weeks to save up that money! Well, well, how glad the dear bishop will be! He's said all the time that you were a good boy."

"Oh, has he?" cried Theo, his face all alight with sudden joy. "I was afraid he'd think I was all bad when he found out how I'd cheated him."

"No, no!" exclaimed Mrs. Martin. "He was grieved over your going off so, and he has tried his best to find you, but you see he didn't know where to look for you."

"Did he try to find me, Mrs. Martin? Oh, I'm so glad! And can I see him now, please?"

The boy's voice trembled with eagerness as he spoke.

The housekeeper's kind face was full of pity and sympathy as she exclaimed, "Why, my boy, didn't you know? The bishop is in California. He went a week ago to stay three months."

All the glad brightness faded from the boy's face as he heard this. He did not speak, but he turned aside, and brushed his sleeve hastily across his eyes. Mrs. Martin laid her hand gently on his shoulder.

"I'm so sorry," she said, "and he will be too, when he knows of your coming. I will write him all about it."

Still the boy stood silent. It seemed to him that he could not bear it. It had not once occurred to him that the bishop might be away, and now there was no possibility of seeing him for three long months. It seemed an eternity to the boy. And to think that he was there--at home--a week ago!

"If they hadn't stole that five dollars from me, I might 'a' seen him last week," the boy said to himself, bitter thoughts of Dick Hunt rising in his heart. At last he turned again to the housekeeper and at the change in his face her eyes filled with quick tears.

He took from his pocket the little roll of money and held it out, saying in a low unsteady voice, "You send it to him--an' tell him--won't you?"

"I'll write him all about it," the housekeeper repeated, "and don't you be discouraged, dear. He'll want to see you just as soon as he gets home, I know he will. Tell me where you live, so I can send you word when he comes."

In a dull, listless voice the boy gave the street and number, and she wrote the address on a slip of paper.

"Remember, Theodore, I shall write the bishop all you have told me, and how you are trying to find the Finney boy and to help others just as he does," said the good woman, knowing instinctively that this would comfort the boy in his bitter disappointment.

He brightened a little at her words but he only said, briefly,

"Yes--tell him that," and then he went sorrowfully away.

Mrs. Martin stood at the window and looked after him as he went slowly down the street, his hands in his pockets and his eyes on the ground, while

Tag, well aware that something was wrong, trotted beside him with drooping ears and tail.

"Tell me that that's a bad boy!" the good woman said to herself. "I know better! I don't care what that Mr. Gibson said. I never took much stock in Mr. Gibson myself, anyhow. He always had something to say against anybody that the bishop took an interest in. There--I wish I'd told Theodore that he was here only as a substitute, and had to leave when the regular secretary was well enough to come back. I declare my heart aches when I think of that poor little fellow's face when I told him that the bishop was gone. Ah well, this is a world of disappointment!" and with a sigh she turned away from the window.

Nan sat in a rocking-chair with Little Brother in her arms, when Theodore opened her door.

"Oh Theo--what is it? What is the matter?" she cried, as she saw his face.

He dropped wearily into a seat and told her in a few words the result of his visit.

"Oh, I am so sorry!" she exclaimed. "And it seems so hard to think that you would have seen the bishop if you hadn't lost that five dollars!"

The boy sighed, but made no reply. He could not talk about it then, and presently he got up and went out.

XI. THEO'S NEW BUSINESS

Theodore went slowly down the stairs, but stopped on the outside steps and stood there with his hands in his pockets looking listlessly up and down the street. There was another big tenement house opposite, and on its steps sat a girl of ten or eleven with a baby in her lap. The baby kept up a low wailing cry, but the girl paid no attention to it. She sat with her head leaning against the house, and seemed to notice nothing about her.

Theodore glanced at her indifferently. His thoughts were still dwelling on his great disappointment--the sorrowful ending of the hopes and longings of so many weeks. It seemed to him that he had now nothing to which to look forward; nothing that was worth working for. Then suddenly there flashed into his mind the words he had heard the bishop speak to a man who came to him one day in great sorrow.

"My life is spoiled," the man had said. "All my hopes and plans are destroyed. What shall I do?"

And the bishop had answered, "My son, you must forget yourself, and your broken hopes and plans, and think of others. Do something for somebody else--and keep on doing."

"That's what he would say to me, I s'pose," thought the boy. "I wonder what I can do. There's Tommy O'Brien, I 'spect he'd be glad 'nough to see most anybody."

He turned and went slowly and reluctantly back up the stairs. He didn't want to see Tommy O'Brien. He didn't want to see anybody just then, but still he went on to Tommy's door. As he approached it, he heard loud, angry voices mingled with the crying of a baby. He knocked, but the noise within continued, and after a moment's pause he pushed open the door and went in.

The three women who lived in the room were all standing with red, angry faces, each trying to outscold the others. Three or four little children, with frightened eyes, were huddled together in one corner, while a baby cried

126

unheeded on the floor, its mother being too much occupied with the quarrel to pay any attention to her child. The women glanced indifferently at Theodore as he entered, and kept on with their loud talk. Theo crossed over to Tommy's cot. The sick boy had pulled his pillow over his head and was pressing it close to his ears to shut out the racket.

"Le'me 'lone!" he exclaimed, as Theodore tried to lift the pillow. His face was drawn with pain and there were dark hollows beneath his heavy eyes. Such a weary, suffering face it was that a great flood of pity surged over Theodore's heart at sight of it. Then Tommy opened his eyes and as he saw who had pulled aside his pillow a faint smile crept around his pale lips.

"Oh!" he cried. "It's you. I thought 'twas some o' them a-pullin' off my piller. Can't you make 'em stop, Tode? They've been a-fightin' off an' on all day." He glanced at the noisy women as he spoke.

"What's the row about?" asked Theo.

"'Cause Mis' Carey said Mis' Green's baby was cross-eyed. Mis' Green got so mad at that that she's been scoldin' 'bout it ever since an' leavin' the baby to yell there by itself on the floor--poor little beggar! Seem's if my head'll split open with all the noise," sighed Tommy, wearily, then he brightened up as he inquired, "What d' you come for, Tode?"

"Just to talk to you a little," replied Theo. "S'pose you get awful tired layin' here all the time, don't ye, Tommy?"

The unexpected sympathy in the voice and look touched the lonely heart of the little cripple. His eyes filled with tears, and he reached up one skinny little hand and laid it on the rough, strong one of his visitor as he answered,

"Oh, you don't know--you don't know anything about it, Tode. I don't b'lieve dyin' can be half so bad's livin' this way. She wishes I'd die. She's said so lots o' times," he nodded toward his aunt, who was one of the women in the room, "an' I wish so too, 'f I've got to be this way always."

"Ain't ye never had no doctor, Tommy?" asked Theo, with a quick catch in his breath as he realised dimly what it would be to have such a life to look forward to.

"No--she says she ain't got no money for doctors," replied the boy, soberly.

"I'll"--began Theodore, then wisely concluding to raise no hopes that might not be realised, he changed his sentence to, "I'll find out if there's a doctor that will come for nothin'. I believe there is one. Can ye read, Tommy?"

The sick boy shook his head. "How could I?" he answered. "Ain't nobody ter show me nothin'."

"Wonder 'f I couldn't," said Theo, thoughtfully. "I c'n tell ye the letters anyhow, an' that'll be better'n nothin'."

A bit of torn newspaper lay on the floor beside the bed. He picked it up and pointed out A, O and S, to Tommy. By the time the little cripple had thoroughly mastered those three letters so that he could pick them out every time, the women had given up their quarrel. Mrs. Green had taken up her baby and was feeding it, and the other women, with sullen faces, had resumed their neglected duties.

"Oh dear! Must you go?" Tommy exclaimed as Theo got off the cot on which he had been sitting. "But you was real good to come, anyhow. When'll ye come again an' tell me some more letters?"

"I'll show ye one ev'ry day if I can get time. Then in three weeks you'll know all the big ones an' some o' the little ones that are just like the big ones. Now don't ye forget them three."

"You bet I won't. I shall say 'em a hundred times 'fore to-morrow," rejoined the little fellow, and his eyes followed his new friend eagerly until the door closed behind him.

As for Theodore himself, half the weight seemed to have been lifted from his own heart as he went down the stairs again.

"I'll run outside a minute 'fore I go to supper," he said to himself. "The air was awful thick in that room. Reckon that's one thing makes Tommy feel so bad."

He walked briskly around two or three squares, and as he came back to the house he noticed that the girl and the baby still sat where he had seen them an hour before. The baby's cry had ceased, but it began again as Theo was passing the two. He stopped and looked at them. The girl's eyes rested on his face with a dull, indifferent glance.

"What makes it cry? Is it sick?" the boy asked, nodding toward the baby.

The girl shook her head.

"What ails it then?"

"Starvin'."

The girl uttered the word in a lifeless tone as if it were a matter of no interest to her.

"Where's yer mother?" pursued the boy.

"Dead."

"An' yer father?"

"Drunk."

"Ain't there nobody to look out for ye?"

Again the girl shook her head.

"Ain't ye had anything to eat to-day?"

"No."

"What d'ye have yesterday?"

"Some crusts I found in the street. Do go off an' le'me 'lone. We're most dead, an' I'm glad of it," moaned the girl, drearily.

"You gi' me that baby an' come along. I'll get ye somethin' to eat," cried Theo, and as the girl looked up at him half doubtfully and half joyfully, he seized the bundle of shawl and baby and hurried with it up to Nan's room, the girl dragging herself slowly along behind him.

Nan cast a doubtful and half dismayed glance at the two strangers as Theodore ushered them in, but the boy exclaimed,

"They're half starved, Nan. We must give 'em somethin' to eat," and when she saw the baby's little pinched face she hesitated no longer, but quickly warmed some milk and fed it to the little one while the girl devoured the bread and milk and meat set before her with a ravenous haste that confirmed what she had said.

Then, refreshed by the food, she told her pitiful story, the old story of a father who spent his earnings in the saloon, leaving his motherless children to live or die as might be. Nan's heart ached as she listened, and Theodore's face was very grave. When the girl had gone away with the baby in her arms, Theo said, earnestly,

"Nan, I've got to earn more money."

"How can you?" Nan asked. "You work so hard now, Theo."

"I must work harder, Nan. I can't stand it to see folks starvin' an' not help 'em. I'll pay you for what these two had you know."

Nan looked at him reproachfully. "Don't you think I want to help too?" she returned. "Do you think I've forgotten that meal you gave Little Brother an' me?"

"That was nothin'. Anyhow you've done lots more for me than ever I did for you," the boy answered, earnestly, "but, Nan, how can rich folks keep their money for themselves when there are people--babies, Nan--starvin' right here in this city?"

"I suppose the rich folks don't know about them," replied the girl, thoughtfully, as she set the table for supper.

"I've got to talk it over with Mr. Scott," Theo said, as he drew his chair up to the table.

"You talk everything over with Mr. Scott now, don't you, Theo?"

"'Most everything. He's fine as silk, Mr. Scott is. He rings true every time, but he ain't"--

He left his sentence unfinished, but Nan knew of whom he was thinking.

The next afternoon Theodore walked slowly through the business streets, with eyes and ears alert, for some opening of which he might take advantage to increase his income. Past block after block he wandered till he was tired and discouraged. Finally he sat down on some high stone steps to rest a bit, and while he sat there a coloured boy came out of the building. He had a tin box and some rags in his hands, and he began in an idle fashion to clean the brass railing to the steps. Theodore fell into conversation with him, carelessly and indifferently at first, but after a little with a sudden, keen interest as the boy began to grumble about his work.

"I ain't a-goin' ter clean these yer ol' railin's many more times," he said. "It's too much work. I c'n git a place easy where the' ain't no brasses to clean, an' I'm a-goin' ter, too. All the office boys hates ter clean brasses."

"What do ye clean 'em with?" Theodore inquired.

The boy held out the tin box. "This stuff an' soft rags. Say--you want ter try it?"

He grinned as he spoke, but to his surprise his offer was accepted. "Gi' me your rags," cried Theo, and he proceeded to rub and polish energetically, until one side of the railings glittered like gold.

"Yer a gay ol' cleaner!" exclaimed the black boy, as he lolled in blissful idleness on the top step. "Now go ahead with the other rail."

But Theodore threw down the rags.

"Not much," he answered. "I've done half your work an' you can do the other half."

"Oh, come now, finish up the job," remonstrated the other. "'Tain't fair not to, for you've made that one shine so. I'll have ter put an extry polish on the other to match it."

But Theodore only laughed and walked off saying to himself,

"Rather think this'll work first-rate."

He went straight to a store, and asked for "the stuff for shining up brass," and bought a box of it. Then he wondered where he could get some clean rags.

"Per'aps Mrs. Hunt'll have some," he thought, "an' anyhow I want to see Jim."

So home he hastened as fast as his feet would carry him.

Good Mrs. Hunt was still a little cool to Theodore, though she could see for herself how steady and industrious he was now, and how much he had improved in every way; but she had never gotten over her first impression of him, founded not only on his appearance and manners when she first knew him, but also on Dick's evil reports in regard to him. Now that Dick himself had gone so far wrong, his mother went about with a heartache all the time, and found it hard sometimes to rejoice as she knew she ought to do in the vast change for the better in this other boy.

"Is Jim here?" Theodore asked when Mrs. Hunt opened the door in response to his knock.

"Yes--what's wanted, Tode?" Jimmy answered for himself before his mother could reply.

"Can you stay out o' school to-morrow?" Theo questioned.

"No, he can't, an' you needn't be temptin' him," broke in the mother, quickly.

"Oh, come now, ma, wait till ye hear what he wants," remonstrated Jimmy, in whose eyes Theo was just about right.

"I wanted him to run my stand to-morrow," said Theodore. "I've got somethin' else to 'tend to. There's plenty o' fellers that would like to run it for me, but ye see I can't trust 'em an' I can trust Jim every time."

Jimmy drew himself up proudly. "Oh, ma, do let me stay out an' do it," he cried, eagerly.

"It's Friday, an' we don't have much to do Fridays anyhow, in our school."

"We-ell, I s'pose then you might stay out just this once," Mrs. Hunt said, slowly, being fully alive to the advantages to Jimmy of such a friendly feeling on Theo's part. She recognized Theodore's business ability, and would have been only too glad to see her own boy develop something of the same kind. She was haunted with a dread that he might become idle and vicious as Dick had done.

"All right, then," Theodore responded, promptly. "You be ready to go down with me at seven o'clock, Jim, an' I'll see you started all right before I leave you. Oh, Mrs. Hunt, there's one more thing I want. Have you any clean old rags?"

"For what?"

"Any kind o' soft white cotton stuff or old flannel will do," replied the boy, purposely leaving her question unanswered. "I'll pay you for 'em, of course, if you let me have 'em."

"Well, I guess I ain't so stingy as all that comes to," exclaimed Mrs. Hunt, sharply. "D'ye want 'em now?"

"I'll come for 'em after supper," answered the boy, thinking that it was best to make sure of them, lest he be delayed for want of them in the morning.

When later that evening, he knocked at her door, Mrs. Hunt had the pieces ready for him, and the next morning, Jimmy was waiting in the hall when Theo came from Nan's room with his big basket, and the two boys went down the street carrying the basket between them. As soon as its contents had been arranged as attractively as possible on the clean white marbled oilcloth with which the stand was covered, and the coffee made and ready to serve, Theo handed Jimmy two dollars in dimes, nickels and pennies, to make change, and set off with the box of paste in his pocket, and the roll of rags under his arm.

Jimmy watched him out of sight, and then with a proud sense of responsibility awaited the appearance of his customers.

Theodore walked rapidly on till he reached the business streets where most of the handsome stores and offices were. Then he slackened his pace and went on slowly, glancing keenly at each building until he came to one that had half a dozen brass signs on the front.

"Here's a good place to make a try," he said to himself, and going into the first office on the ground floor he asked as politely as he knew how,

"Can I shine up your brass signs for you?"

There were several young men in the outer office. One of them answered carelessly, "Yes indeed, shine 'em up, boy, and see 't you make a good job of it."

"I will that, sir," responded Theodore, blithely, and set to work with a will.

There had been much wet weather and the signs were badly discoloured. It took hard, steady rubbing for nearly an hour to get them into good shining order, but Theodore worked away vigourously until they gleamed and glittered in the morning sunlight. Then he went again into the office.

"I've finished 'em, sir," he said to the young man to whom he had spoken before, "an' I think I've made a good job of it. Will you step out an' see what you think?"

"Not at all necessary. If you're satisfied, I am," replied the man, bending over his desk and writing rapidly.

Theodore waited in silence. The young man wrote on. Finally he glanced up and remarked in a tone of surprise,

"Oh, you here yet? Thought you'd finished your job."

"I have done my part. I'm waitin' for you to do yours," replied the boy.

"Mine? What's my part, I'd like to know?" demanded the young man, sharply.

"To pay me for my work." replied Theo, promptly, but with a shadow falling on his face.

"Pay you? Well, if this isn't cheeky! I didn't agree to pay you anything."

"But you knew that I expected to be paid for my work," persisted the boy, the angry colour rising in his cheeks.

"You expected--pshaw! Young man, you've had a lesson that is well worth the time and labour you've expended," remarked the clerk in a tone of great dignity. "Hereafter you will know better than to take anything for granted in business transactions. Good-morning," and he turned his back on the boy and began to write again.

Theodore glanced around the room to see if there was any one on his side, but two of the other clerks were grinning at his discomfiture, and the others pretended not to know anything about the affair. He saw now that he had been foolish to undertake the work as he had done, but he realised that it would not help his case to make a fuss about it. All the same he was unwilling to submit without a protest.

"Next time I'll take care to make my bargain with a gentleman," he said, quietly.

He saw a singular change in the expression of the clerk's face at these words, and as he turned sharply about to leave the office he almost ran into a tall, grey-haired man who had just entered.

"Stop a bit, my boy. I don't understand that remark of yours. What bargain are you going to make with a gentleman?"

The tone of authority, together with the disturbed face of one clerk and the quite evident amusement of the others, suddenly enlightened Theodore.

He knew instinctively that this man was master here and in a few quick sentences he told what had happened.

The gentleman listened in silence, but his keen, dark eyes took note of the flushed face of one clerk and the amused smiles of his companions.

"Is this boy's story true, Mr. Hammond?" he asked, sternly.

Mr. Hammond could not deny it "It was only a joke, sir," he said, uneasily.

"A joke, was it?" responded his employer. "I am not fond of such jokes." Then he turned again to the boy and inquired, "How much is due you for cleaning the signs?"

"I don't know. I'm just starting in in this business, an' I'm not sure what I ought to charge. Can you tell me, sir?"

The gentleman smiled down into the young face lifted so frankly to his.

"Why, no," he answered, gravely, but with a twinkle in his eyes. "I believe our janitor usually attends to the signs."

"Guess he don't attend to 'em very well, for they were awful dirty," remarked the boy. "Took 'me 'most an hour to shine 'em up. Did you notice 'em, sir, as you came in?"

"No, I did not. I'll look at them now," and Theodore followed the gentleman out to the steps.

"Well, you have made a good job of it, certainly," the gentleman said. "The signs haven't shone like that since they were first put there. Quite a contrast to the others on the building. Come back into the office a moment."

He went back to Mr. Hammond's desk and again Theodore followed.

"Mr. Hammond," said the gentleman, quietly, "you are willing of course to pay for your joke. The boy has done his work extremely well. I think he ought to have half a dollar for it."

With anything but a happy expression, Mr. Hammond drew from his pocket a half dollar and handed it to Theodore, who said, not to the clerk, but to the gentleman, "Thank you, sir," and left the office.

But he did not leave the building. He went to the owner of every brass sign in or on the building and asked to be allowed to make every other sign look as well as those of T.S. Harris, which he had just polished.

Now, T.S. Harris was the owner of the building and the occupants of the other offices considered that it would be wise to follow his example in this matter, so the result was that Theodore spent all the morning over the signs on that one building, and Mr. Harris having set the price, he received twenty-five cents for each sign. He was just putting a finishing rub on the last one when the janitor discovered what had been going on. He came at the boy in a great rage for he wanted no one to have anything to do with the care of the building except those whom he chose to hire.

"You take your traps an' clear out o' this now, an' don't you ever dare to show your face here again," he shouted, angrily. "If I catch ye here again I'll kick ye down the stairs!"

"P'raps Mr. Harris will have a word to say about that," replied Theodore, coolly, for in one and another of the offices he had picked up enough to convince him that the word of Mr. Harris was law in that building. Then he added, in a much more friendly tone,

"Now, look here, mister. You're too busy a man to be cleaning signs-- 'course you are. You've got to hire somebody t' do it an' the' won't anybody do it better or fer less money 'n I will. I'm a-goin' to make a reg'lar business of cleanin' brasses all 'round this neighbourhood, an' if you'll stan' by me an' help me fix it all right with the other bosses 'bout here--I'll see 't you don't lose anythin' by it."

The janitor's fierce frown had slowly faded as the boy spoke. Nothing pleased him so much as to be considered a person of influence, and had Theodore been ever so shrewd he could have adopted no other line of argument that would so quickly and effectually have changed an enemy into a friend as did this that he hit upon merely by chance. The man stepped down to the sidewalk and looked up at the signs with a critical air.

"Wai'," he answered, slowly, "I ain't a-goin' to deny that you've done your work well--yes a sight better'n any of the lazy rascals I've been hiring, an' if you could be depended on now, I d'know but what I might's well give the work to you as to anybody else. Of course, as you say, 'tain't my place to do servant's work like brass cleanin'."

"Of course not," assented Theo, promptly.

"But then," the man went on, "if I should speak for ye t' the janitors of the other buildings 'long here, 'n' get ye a big line o' custom, 'course I sh'ld have a right t' expect a--er--a sort o' commission on the profits, so to speak?"

"Oh!" replied Theodore, rather blankly. "What is a commission, anyhow?"

The man explained.

"And how much of a commission would you expect?" questioned the boy.

The janitor made a mental calculation. Here on this one building, the boy had cleaned seven signs. That made a dollar and seventy-five cents that he had earned in one morning. Of course he would not often get so much out of one building, but the man saw that there were good possibilities in this line of work.

"S'pose we say ten per cent.--ten cents out of every dollar?" he ventured, with a keen glance at the boy.

"You mean ten per cent, on all the work that I get through you?" Theo replied.

"Oh no--on all the work of this sort that you do. That's no more'n fair since you'll owe your start to me."

"Not much! I owe my start to myself, an' I'll make no such bargain as that," answered Theo, decidedly. "I'm willin' to give you ten per cent. on all that I get through you, but not a cent more. You see I'm bound to put this thing through whether you help me or not," he added, quietly.

The janitor saw that he had been too grasping and hastened to modify his demands lest he lose his commissions altogether.

"Well, well," he said, soothingly, "we won't quarrel over a little difference like that. Let it be as you say, ten per cent. on all the jobs I get for ye, an' there's the janitor of the Laramie Building on the steps this minute. Come along with me an' I'll give ye a start over there—or, first—ain't there a little matter to attend to," he added, with an insinuating smile. "You'll settle your bills fast as they come due, of course, an' you've got a snug little sum out of my building here."

"Yes, but no thanks to you for that," replied Theo, but as the man's face darkened again, he added, "but never mind, I'll give you the commission on this work since it's in your building," and he handed eighteen cents to the janitor, who slipped it into his pocket with an abstracted air as if unconscious of what he was doing.

The result of the man's recommendation to his brother janitor was that Theodore secured the promise of all the brass cleaning in the Laramie Building also, and that with one or two small jobs kept him busy until dark when he went home with a light heart and with the sum of three dollars and fourteen cents in his pocket. To be sure he had worked hard all day to earn it, but Theodore never had been lazy and he was willing enough to work hard now.

He carried home some oranges as a special treat that night, for now he took his supper regularly with Nan who was glad to make a return in this fashion for the help he was continually giving her in carrying out her food supplies, as well as many other ways.

As they arose from the supper-table, Theodore said, "I'll go across an' see how Jimmy got on to-day, at the stand," but even as he spoke there came a low knock at the door and there stood Jimmy--no longer proud and happy as he had been in the morning, but with red eyes and a face full of trouble.

"Why, Jimmy, what's the matter?" cried Nan and Theo, in one voice.

"Come in," added Nan, kindly pulling him in and gently pushing him toward a chair.

Jimmy dropped into it with an appealing glance at Theo.

"I'm--I'm awful sorry, Tode," he began. "But I--I couldn't help it, truly I couldn't." He rubbed his sleeve hastily across his eyes as he spoke.

"But what is it, Jimmy? I'm sure you did the best you could whatever is wrong, but do tell us what it is," exclaimed Theodore, half laughing and half impatient at the uncertainty.

"'Twas that mean ol' Carrots," began Jimmy, indignantly. "I was sellin' things off in fine style, Tode, an' Carrots, he came along an' he said he wanted three san'wiches in a paper. I put 'em up fer him, an' then he asked fer six doughnuts an' some gingerbread, an' a cup o' coffee--an' he wanted 'em all in a paper."

"Not the coffee, Jimmy," said Nan, laughingly, as the boy stopped to take breath.

"No, 'course not the coffee. He swallered that an' put in a extry spoonful o' sugar too, but he wanted all the rest o' the things in a paper bag, an' I did 'em up good for him, an' then he asked me to tie a string 'round 'em, an' I got down under the stand for a piece of string, an' when I found it, an' looked up--don't you think Tode--that rascal was streakin' it down the street as fast's he could go, an' I couldn't leave the stand to run after him, an' 'course the' wasn't any p'lice 'round, an' so I had to let him go. I'm awful sorry, Theo, but I couldn't help it."

"'Course you couldn't, Jimmy. And is that all the trouble?"

"Yes, that's 'nough, ain't it?" answered Jimmy, mournfully. "He got off with more'n forty cents worth o' stuff--the old pig! I'll fix him yet!"

"Well, don't worry any more over it, Jimmy. Losin' th' forty cents won't break me, I guess," said Theo, kindly.

Jimmy brightened up a little, but the shadow again darkened his face as he said, anxiously, "I s'pose you won't never trust me to run the stand again?"

"Trust you, Jimmy? Well, I guess I will. No danger of your trusting Carrots again, I'm sure."

"Not if I know myself," responded Jimmy, promptly, and Theo went on,

"I s'pose your mother wouldn't want you to stay out of school mornin's for a week or two?"

Jimmy looked at him with sparkling eyes.

"Do you mean"--he began, breathlessly, and then paused.

"I mean that I may want you to run the stand for me all next week, as well as to-morrow," Theo answered.

"Oh--ee! That's most too good to b'lieve," cried the little fellow. "Say! I think you're--you're prime, Tode. I must go an' tell ma," and he dashed out of the door, his face fairly beaming with delight.

"It's worth while to make anybody so happy, isn't it, Theo?" Nan said, then she added, thoughtfully, "Do you think the brass-cleaning will take all your time, so you can't be at the stand any more?"

"Just at first it will. Maybe I shall fix it differently after a while," he answered.

On his way to the business district the next morning, he stopped and bought a blank book and a pencil, and wherever he cleaned a sign or a railing that day, he tried to make a regular engagement to keep the brasses in good condition. If he secured a promise of the work by the month he made a reduction on his price, and every business man--or janitor who regularly engaged him, was asked to write his own name in the new blank book. Not on the first page of the book, however. That the boy kept blank until about the time when Mr. Harris had come to his office the day before.

At that hour, Theodore was waiting near the office door, and there Mr. Harris found him as he came up the steps.

"Good-morning, sir," said Theo, pulling off his cap with a smile lighting up his plain face.

"Good-morning," returned the gentleman. "Have you found something else to polish up here to-day?"

"No, sir, but I wanted to ask you if you would sign your name here in my book," the boy replied.

Mr. Harris looked amused. "Come into my office," he said, "and tell me what it is that you want."

Theodore followed him across the outer office to the private room beyond. The clerks cast curious glances after the two, and Hammond scowled as he bent over his desk.

"Now let me see your book," said Mr. Harris, as the door of the office swung silently behind them.

Theo laid his rags and paste box on the carpet, and then put the blank book on the desk as he said, earnestly,

"You see, sir, I'm trying to work up a reg'lar business, an' so I want the business men I work for to engage me by the month to take care of their brass work--an' I guess I did learn a lesson here yesterday, for to-day I've asked every gentleman who has engaged me to sign his name in this book-- See?"

He turned over the leaves and showed three names on the second page.

"And you want my name there, too? But I haven't engaged you. I only gave you a job yesterday."

"But your janitor has engaged me," answered Theodore, quickly.

"Well, then, isn't it the janitor's name that you want?"

"Oh, no, sir," cried the boy, earnestly. "Nobody knows the janitor, but I guess lots o' folks know you, an' your name would make others sign--don't you see?"

Mr. Harris laughed. "I see that you seem to have a shrewd business head. You'll make a man one of these days if you keep on. And you want my name on this first page?" he added, dipping his pen into the inkstand.

"Yes, because you was my first friend in this business," replied Theodore.

Mr. Harris glanced at him with that amused twinkle in his eye, but he signed his name on the first page.

Then he said, "I wish you success in your undertaking, and here's a trifle for a send-off." He held out a silver dollar as he spoke, but Theodore did not take it.

"Thank ye, sir," he said, gratefully; "you've been real good to me, but I can't take any money now, 'cept what I earn. I c'n earn all I need."

"So?" replied Mr. Harris, "you're independent. Well, I like that, but I'll keep this dollar for you, and if you ever get in a tight place you can come to me for it."

"Thank you, Mr. Harris," said the boy again. "I won't forget, but I hope I won't need it," and then he picked up his belongings and left the office. As he passed Mr. Hammond's desk, he said, "Good-morning, sir," but the clerk pretended not to hear.

All through the next week and for weeks after, Theodore spent his time from nine to five o'clock, cleaning brasses and making contracts for the regular care of them, until he had secured as much work as he could attend to himself.

Meantime, Jimmy Hunt had taken entire charge of the stand and was doing well with it. Theo gave him four-fifths of the profits and he was perfectly satisfied, and so was his mother, who found his earnings a welcome addition to the slim family income, and it was so near the end of the school term that she concluded it did not matter if Jimmy did stay out the few remaining weeks.

But busy as Theodore was, he still found time to carry out what Nan cooked for the people in the two houses, as well as to drop in on one and another of his many neighbours every evening--for by this time the night school had closed for the season. His Saturday evenings were still spent at the flower stand, and now that blossoms were more plentiful, he received more and better ones in payment for his work, and his Sunday morning visits to the different rooms were looked forward to all the week by many of those to whom he went, and hardly less so by himself, for the boy was learning by glad experience the wonderful joy that comes from giving happiness to others. When he saw how the flowers he carried to stuffy, dirty, crowded rooms, were kept and cherished and cared for even until they were withered and dead--he was sure that his little flower mission was a real blessing.

Before the hot weather came, Tommy O'Brien was carried away out of the noisy, crowded room to the Hospital for Incurables. Theo had brought one of the dispensary doctors to see the boy, and through the doctor's efforts and those of Mr. Scott, Tommy had been received into the hospital. He had never been so comfortable in his brief life as he was there, but at first he was lonely, and so Theodore went once or twice a week to see him, and he never failed to save out some flowers to carry to Tommy on Sunday.

But, however full Theodore's time might be, and however busy his hands, he never forgot the search for Jack Finney. His eyes were always watching for a blue-eyed, sandy-haired boy of sixteen, and he made inquiries for him everywhere. Three times he heard of a boy named Finney, and sought him out only to be disappointed, for the first Jack Finney he found was a little chap of ten or eleven, and the next was a boy of sixteen, but with hair and eyes as black as a Jew's--and besides, it turned out that his name wasn't Finney at all, but Findlay; and the third time, the boy he found was living at home with his parents, so Theo knew that no one of the three was the boy of whom he was in search and although he did not in the least give up the matter, he came to the conclusion at last that his Jack Finney must have left the city.

Mr. Scott interested himself in the search because of his great interest in Theodore, and he went to the reform school and the prison, but the name he sought was on neither record.

Although Theodore said nothing to any one about it, he was also on the lookout for another boy, and that boy was Carrots. Ever since Carrots had stolen the food from the stand, Theo had wanted to find him. More than once he had caught a glimpse in the streets of the lank figure and the frowzy red head, but Carrots had no desire to meet Theo and he took good care to keep out of his way.

XII. NAN FINDS FRIENDS

So the spring days slipped away until March and April were gone and the middle of May had come. Theodore was counting the days now, for it was in May that the bishop was to return--so Mrs. Martin had told him--and the boy began to watch eagerly for the word that the housekeeper had promised to send him. So full of this were his thoughts and so busy was he with his work for himself and for others, that he spent much less time than usual with Nan and Little Brother.

About this time there was a week of extremely hot weather. One day toward the close of this week as Theodore was passing Mrs. Hunt's door, she called him in.

"You'd better come here for your supper to-night," she said.

Theodore looked at her with a quick, startled glance.

"Why--where's Nan?" he inquired.

"Nan's in her room, but she can't get you any supper to-night. She's sick. I've seen for weeks past that Nan was overworkin' with all that cooking she's been doin', and to-day she just gave out--an' she's flat on her back now."

Theodore was silent in blank dismay. Until that moment he had not realised how much he had come to depend upon Nan.

"Has she had a doctor, or anything?" he asked, in such a troubled voice that Mrs. Hunt could not but be sorry for him.

"No, I offered to send Jimmy for a doctor, but she said she only wanted to rest, but I tell you what, Theo, she ain't goin' to get much rest in that room, hot's an oven with the constant cooking, an' what's more that baby can't stand it neither."

"I'll go an' see her," replied the boy, slowly, "an'--I guess I don't want any supper to-night, Mrs. Hunt."

"Yes, you do want supper, too, Theodore. You come back here in half an hour an' get it, an' look here--Don't worry Nan, talkin' 'bout her being sick," Mrs. Hunt called after him in a low voice, as he turned toward the girl's door.

It seemed strange enough to Theodore to see bright, energetic Nan lying with pale face and idle hands on the bed. She smiled up at the boy as he stood silent beside the bed finding no words to say.

"I'm only tired, Theo," she said, gently. "It has been so hot to-day, and Little Brother fretted so that I couldn't get through my work so well as usual."

"He's sick too," answered Theodore, gravely.

Nan turned her head to look at the little white face on the pillow beside her.

"Yes, he's sick. Oh Theo"--and then the girl covered her face with her hands, and Theodore saw the tears trickling through her fingers.

"Don't Nan, don't!" he cried, in a choked voice, and then he turned and ran out of the room and out of the house. Straight to his teacher he went, sure of finding there sympathy, and if possible, help.

He was not disappointed. Mr. Scott listened to what he had to say, and wrote a note to a friend of his own who was a physician, asking him to see Nan and the baby at his earliest convenience. Then having comforted Theodore, and compelled him to take some supper, Mr. Scott sent him away greatly refreshed, and proceeded to talk the matter over with his aunt, Mrs. Rawson.

"Those two children ought to be sent away into the country, Aunt Mary," he began.

"Nan and Theodore, do you mean?"

"No, no! Theodore's all right. He's well and strong. I mean Nan and her little brother. Aunt Mary, it would make your heart ache to see such a girl

147

as that working as she has worked, and living among such people. I wish you would go and see the child."

"I'll try to go to-morrow, Allan. I've been intending to ever since you told me about her, but the days do slip away so fast!" answered the lady.

But she found time to go the next day, and the first sight of Nan's sweet face was enough to make her as deeply interested in the two as her nephew had long been.

"But what an uncomfortable place for a sick girl!" Mrs. Rawson thought, as she glanced at the shutterless windows through which the sun was pouring, making the small room almost unbearably hot, although there was no fire in the stove. She noticed that the place was daintily clean and neat, though bare as it well could be, but noisy children were racing up and down the stairways and shouting through the halls, making quiet rest impossible. Mrs. Rawson's kind heart ached as she looked from the room to the pure face of the girl lying there with the little child beside her.

"She must be a very unusual girl to look like that after living for months in this place," she thought to herself.

While she was there the doctor came, and when he went away, Mrs. Rawson went with him that she might tell him what she knew about the girl's life and learn what he thought of the case.

"It is a plain case of overwork," he said. "From what you tell me the girl has been doing twice as much as she was able to do, and living in that little oven of a room with nothing like the fresh air and exercise she should have had, and very likely not half enough to eat. The baby seems extremely delicate. Probably it won't live through the summer, and a good thing too if there's no one but the girl to provide for them. What they need is--to go straight away into the country and stay there all summer, or better yet, for a year or two, but I suppose that is out of the question."

"I must see what can be done, doctor. Such a girl as that surely ought not to be left to struggle along unfriended."

148

"No, but there are so many such cases. Well, I hope something can be done for her. I'll call and see her again to-morrow, but medicine is of little use in a case like this," the doctor replied.

Mrs. Rawson was not one to "let the grass grow under her feet," when she had anything to do, and she felt that she had something to do in this case. She thought it over as she went home, and before night she had written to a relative in the country--a woman who had a big farm and a big heart--to ask if she would board Nan and her little brother for the summer. She described the two, and told how bravely the girl had battled with poverty and misfortune until her strength had failed. The letter went straight from the warm heart of the writer to that of her friend and the response was prompt.

"Send those two children right to me, and if rest and pure air and plenty of wholesome food are what they need, please God, they shall soon be strong and well. They are surely His little ones, and you know I am always ready and glad to do His work."

Such was the message that Mrs. Rawson read to her nephew two days after her visit to Nan, and his face was full of satisfaction as he listened to it.

"Nothing could be better," he said. "It will be a splendid place for those children, and it will be a good thing too for Mrs. Hyde to have them there."

"Yes, I think so," replied Mrs. Rawson, "but now the question is--will Nan consent to go? From what little I have seen of her I judge that she will not be at all willing to accept help from strangers."

"She will shrink from it, perhaps, for herself, but for the sake of that little brother I think she will consent to go. Theo tells me that she has been exceedingly anxious about the child for weeks past," answered Mr. Scott.

"Well, I'll go to-morrow and see if I can prevail upon her to accept this offer, but Allan, one thing you must do, if Nan does consent to go--and that is, you must break it to Theodore. It's going to be a blow to him, to have those two go away from the city. He'll be left entirely alone."

"So he will. I hadn't thought of that. I must think it over and see what can be done for him. He certainly must not stay there, with no place but that dark little closet in which he sleeps," replied the gentleman.

Mrs. Rawson's kindly sympathy and gentle manners had quickly won Nan's confidence and the girl welcomed her warmly when she appeared in the little room the next morning. She found Nan sitting by the open window, with her pale little brother in her arms.

"Oh, I'm ever so much better," she said, in reply to Mrs. Rawson's inquiries. "The doctor's medicine helped me right away, but I don't feel very strong yet--not quite well enough to begin my cooking again. I'm going to begin it to-morrow," she added.

"Indeed, you'll not do any cooking to-morrow, Nan," said the lady, decidedly. "You're not fit to stand over the stove or the mixing board, and besides, it would make the room too hot for the baby."

Nan glanced anxiously at the little face on her arm.

"I can carry him in to Mrs. Hunt's. He's no trouble, and she's always willing to keep him," she answered.

"Now, my child, I want you to listen to me," Mrs. Rawson began, and went on to tell the girl about the plans she had made for her and her little brother.

Nan listened, with the colour coming and going in her face.

"It is so good--so kind of you to think of this," she exclaimed, earnestly, "and I'd love to go. Mrs. Rawson, you don't know how I hate living in a place like this," she shuddered, as she spoke, "and it would be like heaven to get away into the sweet clean country, with good people--but I can't go unless there is something I can do there. I couldn't go and live on charity, you know."

"It wouldn't be charity, Nan; it would be love," answered Mrs. Rawson, gently. "Mrs. Hyde keeps one room in her house always ready for any guest whom the Lord may send her and I think He is sending you there now. Remember, my child, you have this dear sick baby to think of, as well as yourself. Nan, the doctor thinks Little Brother will not live through the summer unless he is taken away from the city."

Nan gave a quick, gasping breath, as she drew the baby closer and bent her face over his. When she looked up again her eyes were wet, and she said, in a low tone,

"If that is so, I can't refuse this kind offer, and I will try to find some way to make it right."

"There's nothing to make right, dear; you've only to go and be just as happy and contented as you can be. I know you will be happy there. You can't help loving Mrs. Hyde. And now, my child, there's another matter." She paused and added, in a low tone, "I had a little girl once, but God took her away from my home. She would have been about your age now if she had staid with me. For her sake, Nan, I want you to let me get a few things that you and the baby will need. Will you, dear?"

Nan was proud. She had never gotten accustomed to poverty and its painful consequences, and she would have preferred to do without, any time, rather than accept a gift from those on whom she had no claim; but she realised that she could not go among strangers with only the few poor garments that she now had, so, after a moment's silence, she answered, in a voice that was not quite steady,

"You are very, very good to me, Mrs. Rawson. I'll try to be good too, only, please don't get a single thing that I can do without."

"Nan, if you had plenty of money and you found a girl who had been left all alone in the world, with no one to do anything for her--would you think it was any wonderful kindness in you to spend a few dollars for her?"

"N--no, of course not. I'd just love to do it," replied Nan, "but"--

"That's enough, then, and now there's only one more thing I have to speak about. I know some girls, who have formed themselves into a band called a

'King's Daughter Circle,' and they meet once a week to sew for somebody who is not able to do her own sewing. I've told these girls a little about you and they want very much to do some sewing for Little Brother and you. Now, would you be willing to let them come here to-morrow afternoon? Would it trouble you?"

The colour rose in Nan's cheeks and her lips trembled, and for a moment she seemed to shrink into herself as she thought what a contrast her poor surroundings would be to these other girls, who lived such different lives from hers, but she saw that Mrs. Rawson was really desirous that they should come, and she was not willing to disappoint one who was doing so much for her; so after a moment's silence she answered,

"Of course they can come, if you think they won't mind too much." She glanced about the room as she spoke.

Mrs. Rawson leaned over and kissed her. "Child," she said, "they know nothing about the trials that come into other lives--like yours. I want them to know you. Don't worry one bit over their coming. They are dear girls and I'm sure you will like them--as sure as I am that they will all love you-- and Nan, one thing more, leave Mr. Scott to tell Theodore about your going."

Then she went away, leaving Nan with many things to think about. She could not help worrying somewhat over the coming of those girls. As she recalled her own old home, she realised how terribly bare and poor her one room would look to these strangers and she shrank nervously from the thought of meeting them. More than once, she was tempted to ask Theo to go to Mrs. Rawson and tell her that the girls could not come there.

Mrs. Rawson went straight from Nan's room to the shopping district, where she purchased simple but complete outfits for Nan and the baby. The under garments and the baby's dresses she bought ready-made and also a neat wool suit for the girl and hats and wraps for both, but she bought enough pretty lawn and gingham to make as many wash dresses as Nan would require, and these she carried home and cut out the next morning. That evening too she sent notes to the members of the circle telling them to meet at her house before one o'clock the next day, which was Saturday.

They came promptly, eleven girls between fifteen and seventeen, each with her sewing implements. Bright, happy girls they were, as Nan might have been, had her life been peaceful and sheltered like theirs, Mrs. Rawson thought, as she welcomed them. "Sit down, girls," she said, "I want to tell you more about my poor little Nan before you see her."

She told the story in such fashion that the warm, girlish hearts were filled with a sweet and tender sympathy for this other girl, and they were eager to do all that they could for her.

Not one of them had ever before been in a tenement house like the one to which Mrs. Rawson led them, and they shrank from the rude children and coarse women whom they encountered in the halls and on the stairs, and pressed closer together, grasping each other's hands.

Nan's face whitened and her thin hands were clasped tightly together as she heard them coming along the hall. She knew it was they, so different were their quiet footsteps from most that passed her door.

Nan opened the door in response to Mrs. Rawson's knock and the girls flocked in, looking so dainty and pretty in their fresh shirt-waists and dimities, and their gay ribbons. As Nan looked at them she was painfully conscious of her own faded calico and worn shoes, and her cheeks flushed, but the girls gave her no time to think of these things. They crowded about her, introducing each other with merry laughter and gay little jokes, seeming to take Nan right in among them as one of themselves, and taking prompt possession of the baby, who wasn't a bit shy, and appeared to like to be passed from one to another, and kissed, and called sweet names.

Nan had borrowed all Mrs. Hunt's chairs, but still there were not enough, and three or four girls gleefully settled themselves on the bed. Every one of them had come with her hands full of flowers, and seeing these, Mrs.

Rawson had brought along a big glass rose bowl, which the girls speedily filled and set in the middle of the table.

A tap at the door announced the arrival of a boy with a box and a bag for Mrs. Rawson, and out of the box she lifted a baby sewing machine, which she fastened to the table. Then from the bag she took the lawn and gingham as she said,

"Now, girls, your tongues can run just as fast as your fingers sew, but remember this tiny machine works very rapidly and you've got to keep it supplied. I'll hem this skirt first."

In an instant every girl had on her thimble, and they all set to work with right good will.

"Can't I do some, too?" said Nan. "I don't want to be the only idle one."

"You can gather some ruffles in a few minutes--as soon as I have hemmed them," answered Mrs. Rawson, smiling to herself, as she saw how bright and interested Nan looked already.

All that long, bright afternoon tongues and needles were about equally busy. Fortunately it was cooler, else the girls would have been uncomfortable in the small room, but as it was, not even Nan gave more than a passing thought to the bare room and its lack of comfort. Indeed, after the first few moments, Nan forgot all about herself and just gave herself up to the delight of being once more a girl among girls. She thought them lovely, every one, and indeed they were lovely to her in every way, for her sweet face and gentle manners had won them all at first sight. How they did chatter! Never before had that room--or indeed any room in that dreary building, held such a company as gathered there that day.

At half-past five there came another rap on the door, and Mrs. Rawson exclaimed, "Put up your sewing, girls. We've business of another sort to attend to now."

The girls looked at her inquiringly as Nan opened the door again.

"Bring them in," called Mrs. Rawson, and a man edged his way gingerly among the girls and set two big baskets and an ice cream freezer beside the table.

"A house picnic! Mrs. Rawson, you're a darling!" called one and another of the girls.

Mrs. Rawson nodded a laughing acknowledgment of the compliment, as she said, "Open the baskets, girls. The dishes are in the round one. I thought Nan might not be prepared for quite such a family party."

With quick, deft fingers the girls swept aside the sewing, unscrewed the little machine, spread a fine damask cloth over the pine table, and on it arranged the pretty green and gold dishes and glasses, putting the big bowl of roses in the centre.

Then from the other basket they took tiny buttered biscuits, three-cornered sandwiches, tied with narrow green ribbons, a dish of chicken salad, and a big loaf of nut cake. All these quite covered the table so that the cream had to be left in the freezer until it was wanted.

How Nan did enjoy that feast! How her eyes shone with quiet happiness as she watched the bright faces and listened to the merry talk; not all merry either, for more than once it touched upon the deep things of life, showing that the girls had thought much, even if their lives had been happy, sheltered ones.

When the feast was ended, the dishes repacked in the basket, and the unfinished work put away, the girls gathered about Nan to say "good-bye," and she wondered how she could have dreaded their coming,--for now it seemed as if she could not let them go. She felt as if all the joyous brightness would vanish with them. The quick young eyes read something of this feeling in her face, and more than one girl left a kiss with her cordial farewell.

The room seemed very still and lonely to Nan when the last flutter of light dresses was gone and the last faint echo of girlish voices and footsteps had died on her eagerly listening ears. She dropped into the rocking-chair and looked about the room, trying to repeople it with those fair, young, friendly faces. She could almost have imagined it all a dream but for the cake and sandwiches and ice cream on the table.

The sight of the fast melting cream suggested another thought to her. Hastily filling a plate with portions of everything on the table, she set it away for Theodore and then went across to Mrs. Hunt's rooms to tell her to come with the children and take all that was left.

The eyes of the children gleamed with delight at sight of the unexpected treat, and they speedily emptied the dishes which their mother then carried home to wash, while the children took back the borrowed chairs.

By this time Nan began to feel very weary, and she threw herself down on the bed with the baby, but she kept in her hand some little scrips of the pretty lawns and ginghams that she had found on the floor. It seemed hardly possible to her that she could be going to have such dresses. Why-- one of the scrips was exactly like a waist that one of those girls had worn. Nan gazed at it with a smile on her lips, a smile that lingered there until it was chased away by the remembrance of Theo's loneliness when she and Little Brother should be far away.

XIII. NAN'S DEPARTURE

Theo was feeling that he needed sympathy about that time, for it seemed to him as if every one that he cared for was to be taken away from him.

Mr. Scott had invited the boy to go with him for a row on the river and then to go home with him to supper. The river was beautiful in the afternoon sunlight, and Theodore enjoyed the row and the friendly talk with his teacher, but he felt a little shy with Mrs. Rawson and was not sorry to find her absent from the supper-table.

When the meal was over Mr. Scott took the boy up to his own room to see some of his curiosities. Theo's quick eyes took silent note of everything, and he mentally decided that some day he would have just such a room as that. He was thinking thus, when Mr. Scott said,

"Theo, you haven't asked me what Dr. Reed thinks about Nan and her little brother."

"She's better to-day--Nan is," exclaimed the boy, quickly.

"Yes, I suppose the medicine has toned her up a little, but the doctor says that she must have a long rest. She has been working too hard."

"Well, she can. I'm earnin' enough now to take care of 'em," interposed the boy.

"Nan would never be content to let you do that, I think, but, Theo, that isn't all."

Theo said nothing, but his anxious eyes asked the question that his lips refused to utter.

Mr. Scott went on, "The doctor says that the baby must go away into the country or--he will die."

Theodore walked quickly to the window, and stood there looking out in silence. After a moment, his teacher crossed the room and laid his arm affectionately over the boy's shoulders.

"Sit down, Theodore," he said, gently, "I want to tell you what we have planned for Nan and the little one."

Then in few words he told of Mrs. Rawson's letter and the reply, describing the beautiful country home to which Nan and the baby were to go.

"You will be glad to think of them in such a place during the hot summer days," he went on, "even though their going leaves you very lonely, as I know it will, Theodore."

"I ought to be glad, Mr. Scott," replied the boy, slowly, as his teacher paused, "an' I am, but ye see you don't know how hard 'tis for a feller to keep straight when he ain't got no home an' nobody to talk to after his work's done at night. Nan--well you know she ain't like the rest o' the folks down our way. She never scolds nor nags at me, but somehow I can't ever look her straight in the eye if I've been doin' anything mean."

"Nan has been a good friend to you, I'm sure, and I think you have been a good friend to her and the baby, Theodore. I know that she will miss you sadly at first, and if she thinks you are to be very lonely without them, I'm afraid she will worry about it and not get as much good from the change as she might otherwise," Mr. Scott added.

The boy drew a long breath. "I won't let her know 't I care much 'bout their goin'," he said, bravely.

"Nan will guess quite enough," answered the gentleman, "but, Theodore, how would you like to come here? Mrs. Rawson has a little room over the L that she seldom uses, and she says that you can sleep there if you like, and pay for it the same that you pay for the dark room that you now have."

The boy's eyes were full of surprise and pleasure as he answered, gratefully, "I'd like that fine!"

"Come on, then, and we'll take a look at the place. It has been used as a storeroom and will, of course, need some fixing up."

As Mr. Scott threw open the door of the L room Theodore stepped in and looked about him with shining eyes. It was a long, low room with windows on three sides. The floor was covered with matting and the walls with a light, cheerful paper.

"This for me!" exclaimed the boy. "Why, Mr. Scott, it's--it's too fine for a chap like me."

"Not a bit, my boy, but I think you can be very comfortable here, and you will know that you have friends close at hand. And now, Theodore, I suppose you will want to get home, for we hope to get Nan away next week."

"So soon!" cried the boy, a shadow falling on the face, a moment before so bright.

"Yes, the sooner the better for the little one's sake," replied Mr. Scott, gravely.

"You've been mighty good to me--an' to Nan," said the boy, simply, and then he went away.

He walked rapidly through the streets, taking no note of what was passing around him, his thoughts were so full of this new trouble, for a great and sore trouble it seemed to him to lose Nan and Little Brother out of his life even for a few weeks. His way led him across the Common, but he hurried along with unseeing eyes until suddenly something bright attracted his attention, and he became aware that it was a shock of rough red hair under a ragged old cap. It was surely Carrots sitting on one of the benches, his eyes gazing moodily across the greensward to the street beyond. He did not notice Theo's approach, but started up quickly, as the latter stopped in front of him.

"Hold on, Carrots--don't clear out. I want to tell you something," cried Theo, hastily, laying a detaining hand on one ragged sleeve.

Carrots looked at him suspiciously. "D'know what yer got ter say ter me," he growled.

"Sit down here, an' I'll tell ye."

Theodore sat down on the bench as he spoke, and after a moment's hesitation the other boy dropped down beside him, but he kept a wary glance on his companion, and was plainly ready to "cut and run" at a moment's notice.

"You look's if you were down on your luck," began Theo, with a glance at the ragged garments, and dilapidated shoes of the other.

"'Course--I'm always down on my luck," responded Carrots, in a tone that implied, "what business is that of yours?"

"Sellin' papers now?"

"Yes, but a feller can't make a livin' out o' that. There's too many kids in the business, an' folks'll buy o' the kids ev'ry time, 'n' give us big fellers the go-by," Carrots said, in a gloomy tone.

"That's so. The little chaps always sell most," assented Theodore. "Why don't you get into some other business, Carrots?"

"Can't--'cause my money's all tied up in railroad stock," retorted Carrots, with bitter sarcasm.

"Carrots, what made ye play such a mean trick on Jim Hunt the other day?" asked Theodore, suddenly.

Carrots grinned. "Hunt's a fool," he answered, "else he wouldn't 'a' give me a chance ter work him so slick."

"Well, I don't think you'll play it on him again. I think you were the fool, Carrots, for you know well enough you can't get such good stuff anywhere else for your money, an' now ye can't go to my stand."

"Got it 'thout money that time," chuckled Carrots, impudently, but still keeping a sharp eye on his companion.

Theo flushed, and his fingers itched to pitch into the boy and give him a good drubbing, but he controlled himself, and said, quietly, "What's the trouble with you, Carrots? Are you too lazy to work, or what?"

The boy's eyes flashed angrily, as he replied, "See here, Tode Bryan--what ye pokin' yer nose int' my business for, anyhow?"

"'Cause I can put you in the way of earnin' honest money if you're willin' to do honest work."

"What sort o' work?" Carrots inquired, suspiciously.

"I'll tell ye 'bout it when I'm sure you're ready to take hold of it, an' not before. See here, Carrots, I've seen you lately loafin' 'round with some o' the meanest fellers in this town, an' if you don't keep away from them you'll find yourself where some of 'em have been a'ready--behind the bars. I mean well by ye, an' if you make up your mind to be a man instead of a tramp an' a loafer, you can come to me, an' I'll give ye a start. Jim Hunt'll tell ye where to find me."

The night shadows were falling now and the street lamps were already lighted, and seeing this, Theodore started up, adding, "It's later'n I thought. I must be off," and he hurried away, leaving Carrots looking after him in a much bewildered state of mind.

Theodore found Nan sitting by the window in the dark. She had rocked the baby to sleep, and was thinking over the happy afternoon that seemed now so like a beautiful dream. She lighted her lamp when Theodore came in, and brought out the food that she had put aside for him, and while he ate she told him of all that had happened. He did not eat much and he was very silent, so silent that at last she paused and said, anxiously,

"You aren't sick, are you, Theo?"

"No," he replied, gravely, "an' Nan, I'm real glad you're goin' to such a nice place." But though he spoke earnestly, there was in his voice a ring of pain that Nan detected instantly, and guessed its cause.

"I'm going to miss you dreadfully, Theo," she said, quickly, "and I don't know what Little Brother will do without you. That's the one thing about it that I don't like--to think of you all alone here with no place to stay evenings."

"Mr. Scott says I can have a room where he lives--at Mrs. Rawson's," answered Theodore. "It's a fine room--bigger'n this, an' it's got checked straw carpet an' three windows."

"Oh, Theo, how glad I am!" cried the girl, delightedly. "That's just splendid. Don't you like it?" she added, as the boy still sat with serious eyes fixed on the floor.

"Like it? The room you mean? Oh yes, it's a grand room, but I don't think I'll go there," he answered, slowly.

The gladness died out of Nan's face. "Oh, Theo, why not?" she exclaimed, in a disappointed tone.

He answered again, slowly, "I think I shall stay here an' take this room o' yours 'stead o' my little one."

"This is ever so much better than yours, of course, an' if you do that you can keep my furniture, and I s'pose you'd be comfortable, but 'twould be lonesome all the same, and I shouldn't think you'd like it half so well as being with Mr. Scott."

"'Course I wouldn't like it half nor quarter so well, Nan, but this is what I've been thinkin'. You know there's a good many boys in these two houses that don't have no place to stay evenin's, 'cept the streets, an' I was thinkin' as I came home to-night, how fine 'twould be if there was a room where they could come an' read an' play games an' talk, kind of a boys' club room, don't ye know, like the one Mr. Scott was tellin' 'bout they're havin' in some places. I think he'll help me get some books an' papers an' games, an' maybe he'll come an' give us a talk sometimes. It would be grand for fellers like Jimmy Hunt that ain't bad yet, but will be if they stay in the streets every evenin'."

"Theo, I think it's a splendid idea, only there ought to be just such a room for the girls. They need it even more than the boys do." Nan hesitated a moment, then added, earnestly, "Theo, I'm proud of you."

Theodore's face was the picture of utter amazement as he gazed at her. "Proud--of me?" he gasped. "I'd like to know what for."

"Well, never mind what for, but I want to say, Theo, what I've thought ever so many times lately. When I first knew you, you were good to Little Brother and me, so good that I can never forget it, but you weren't"--

"I was meaner'n dirt," interposed the boy, sorrowfully.

"No, but you'd never had any chance with nobody to teach you or help you, and I used to hate to have you touch Little Brother, because I thought you were not good."

"I wasn't," put in Theodore, sadly.

"But since you came back from the bishop's you've been so different, and it seems to me you're always trying to help somebody now. Theo--if Little Brother lives, I hope he'll be like you." Theodore stared at her in incredulous silence. "Like me. Little Brother like me," he whispered, softly, to himself, the colour mounting in his cheeks. Then he arose and walked over to the bed where the child lay, with one small hand thrown out across the bedclothes. The soft, golden hair lay in pretty rings on the moist forehead, but the little face looked waxen white.

Theodore stood for a moment looking down at the baby, then suddenly he stooped and kissed the outstretched hand, and then without another word he went away.

Nan's eyes were full of tears as she looked after him.

"How he does love Little Brother," she thought. "He's going to miss him awfully."

Monday was a busy day for Mrs. Rawson. She had engaged a seamstress to finish off Nan's dresses, and having seen the woman settled to her work, she set off herself for the tenement house, a boy going with her to carry a small valise.

She found Nan busy baking bread. The place was very warm and the girl looked flushed and tired. Mrs. Hunt had carried the baby off to her cooler rooms.

"Nan, child, you've not taken up the cooking again?" exclaimed Mrs. Rawson.

"I had to do some--not very much," replied the girl, gently.

"But, my dear, I thought you understood that we didn't want you to do this any more."

Nan only smiled as she set the last loaf in the oven.

The lady went on, "Nan--we want you to go away to-morrow."

Nan looked up with startled eyes. "So soon!" she exclaimed as Theodore had done.

"Why should there be any delay about it? Every day that you stay here is so much actual loss to you and to the baby, too," added Mrs. Rawson.

With a bewildered air Nan dropped into a chair, saying, hesitatingly,

"But how can I get ready to go to-morrow?"

"Easily enough, if you let the cooking go. I was wondering as I came along what you would do with your furniture."

To Mrs. Rawson's eyes the few poor bits of furniture looked worthless enough, but she realised that it would seem quite otherwise to the girl who had bought them with her own hard earnings.

But now Nan looked up with shining eyes and in eager words told of Theodore's plan and the lady's face brightened as she listened.

"It's a fine plan," she replied, heartily, "and it means a deal for such a boy as Theodore to have thought of it."

"And when he might have gone to your house, too," added Nan, softly. "Mrs. Rawson, he'll be very lonely when Little Brother is gone."

"Yes, he'll miss you both sadly, but Nan, you mustn't worry about Theodore. Mr. Scott loves the boy and will look out for him, you may be sure of that. But now we must talk about your journey. I've brought the things that I thought you would need on the way, and I'd like you to try on this dress."

She lifted the pretty wool suit from the valise as she spoke, and Nan began to take off her faded calico. The colour rose in her face as she did so, for she hated to have Mrs. Rawson see her poor under garments, but the lady seemed not to notice, as she chatted away about the dress.

"Fits you beautifully. I was sure it would, for I had all the measurements. I don't believe you will need to carry many of the things you have, for there are plenty of the new ones," she said. "I put into this little valise everything that will be needed for the journey, and the other things can go with mine."

Nan looked up quickly, crying out joyfully, "Oh, Mrs. Rawson, are you going with us?"

"To be sure. Did you suppose I meant for you to travel alone with a sick baby? I'm going to stay a week."

"That's lovely!" exclaimed the girl, with a sigh of relief. "I did dread to go among entire strangers alone."

"Mrs. Hyde won't be a stranger two minutes after you meet her. You couldn't help loving her if you should try. Now then, let me see. You are to be ready at half past nine to-morrow. The train goes at 10:15. I'll stop here for you. Now, child, don't work any more to-day. Just rest so that you can enjoy the journey. Oh, there's one thing I came near forgetting--shoes. Those will have to be fitted. Can you come with me now and get them?"

"Yes, if Mrs. Hunt can see to my baking," Nan replied.

165

Mrs. Hunt was very ready to do so, and Nan and her new friend were soon in a car on their way to the shoe store.

When she returned to her room alone, the girl took out the pretty serviceable garments from the valise and examined them all with mingled pain and pleasure. It was a delight to her to have once more such clothing as other girls wore, but to receive them from strangers, even such kind strangers as Mrs. Rawson and the girls, hurt Nan more than a little. But she did not feel quite the same about the dainty garments for her little brother. Over those her eyes shone with satisfaction. She could not resist the desire to see how he would look in them, and when he was dressed she carried him in for Mrs. Hunt to admire, and the two praised and petted the little fellow to their hearts' content.

Theodore had looked forward to a quiet evening with Nan and the baby-- that last evening that they were to spend together for so long--but it proved to be anything but a quiet one. It had leaked out that Nan was going away, and all through the evening the women and girls in the house were coming to say "good-bye." Nan had not expected this, for she had never had much to do with any of them, and it touched her deeply when in their rough fashion they wished her a pleasant summer and hoped that the baby would come back well and strong.

Theodore sat silent in a corner through all these leave-takings, and some of the women, as they went back to their own rooms, spoke of the loneliness the boy would feel without the baby that they all knew he loved so dearly.

When the last caller had departed, Theodore stood up and held out a little purse to Nan.

"Ain't much in it, but I want ye to use it for anything he wants," the boy said, with a gesture toward the child.

Nan hesitated. She would not have taken it for herself, but she knew that it would hurt Theo sadly, if she refused his gift, so she took it, saying, "You've been so good to him always, Theo. I shan't let him forget you ever."

"No--don't," muttered the boy, and unable to trust himself to say more, he turned away in silence, and went to his own room. The little purse he had given Nan contained five dollars.

"The dear boy! How good he is to us," Nan murmured, as she put the bill back into it, "but I hope I shall not need to use this."

Theodore ran in the next morning for a hasty good-bye before he went out to his work. He had waited purposely until the last moment, so that his leave-taking might be a brief one, and he said so little, and said that little so coldly that a stranger might have thought him careless and indifferent, but Nan knew better. Now that the time of departure was so close at hand, she shrank nervously from it and almost wished she had refused to go, but still she dressed Little Brother and herself in good season, and was all ready when at nine thirty, promptly, Mrs. Rawson appeared. The lady gave a satisfied glance at the two, and then insisted upon carrying the baby downstairs herself, while one of the Hunt children followed with Nan's valise. A cab was waiting at the door, and cabs being rarities in that locality, a crowd of curious children stood gaping at it, and waiting to see Nan and the baby depart in it.

"It is going to be a warm day. I shall be glad when we are fairly off," Mrs. Rawson said, with an anxious glance at the baby's face, as the cab rattled over the rough stones.

As the little party entered the station, there was a flutter of light raiment and bright ribbons, and Nan found herself fairly surrounded by the eleven King's Daughters. They took possession of the baby, who brightened up wonderfully at the sight of them, and they seized the valise and Mrs. Rawson's handbag, and they trooped altogether through the great station to the waiting train, and instead of saying, "Can't go through yet, ladies-- not till the train's made up," the gatekeeper smiled in genial fashion into their bright faces and promptly unlocked the gate for them. That was because one of them was the daughter of a railroad official, but Nan didn't know that.

The train was not all ready, but two of the parlor cars were there, and into one of these the girls climbed, and then they found the seats belonging to Mrs. Rawson and Nan, and put the extra wraps up in the rack for them and pushed up the window, and did everything else that they could think of for the comfort of the travellers.

Then one of them pinned a great bunch of deliciously fragrant violets to Nan's dress, and another fastened a tiny silver cross above the violets, as she whispered,

"We've made you a member of our circle, Nan, dear, and this is our badge."

And then Nan noticed that every one of the girls wore the tiny, silver cross somewhere about her dress. She wondered what it meant and determined to ask Mrs. Rawson later, but she could not talk much just then--she was too happy with all those dear girls about her, chattering to her and counting her in with themselves.

At last there was a rumble and a jar, and people began to fill up the seats in the car and one of the girls looked at her watch and exclaimed, "We must say 'good-bye' girls, or we shall be carried off."

"Wouldn't it be fun if we could all go too, and stay for the week with Mrs. Rawson?" cried another.

"Yes, indeed. If it weren't for school we might have done it."

"Now remember, Nan, we're all going to write to you because you belong to our circle," whispered another, and then, some with a kiss, and some with a warm handshake, they said, "good-bye," and hastened out of the car and stood on the platform outside the car windows, calling out more farewells and last words, and waving hands and handkerchiefs, until the train drew out of the station.

Then Nan settled back in her comfortable seat with a happy light in her dark eyes.

"I didn't suppose there were any such girls in all the world, Mrs. Rawson," she said; "girls who would be so dearly kind to a stranger like me."

"They certainly are dear girls. I think myself that there are not many like them," Mrs. Rawson answered. "Some of them have been in my Sunday-school class ever since they were nine years old."

"Perhaps that accounts for it," Nan answered, shyly, with one of her quick, bright smiles. Then she turned to look out of the window and her face changed, for there on a fence, close beside the track, stood Theodore, eagerly scanning the windows as the train went by. Nan snatched up Little Brother and held him to the window, and a smile broke over the boy's face as he waved his hat in response. Then the train gathered speed and flew on, and the boy went slowly back to his work.

It was nearly sunset when the station where the travellers were to stop, was reached. Nan's heart began to beat fast and she glanced around somewhat anxiously as she stepped on to the platform, but the next moment she found herself looking into Mrs. Hyde's face, and from that instant all her fears and anxieties vanished.

Mrs. Hyde had no children of her own, but the very spirit of motherliness seemed to look out of her eyes, and she took the two strangers into her heart at sight. The baby, wearied with the long journey had been fretting for the last hour, but no sooner did he find himself in Mrs. Hyde's arms, than he settled down comfortably and went to sleep and slept soundly through the three mile drive from the station.

Mrs. Hyde did not say much to Nan during the drive, only by an occasional word or smile, showing her that she was not forgotten, while the two ladies talked together, but at last she laid her firm, strong hand lightly on the girl's fingers, saying,

"Look, dear--you are almost home."

And Nan looked with happy eyes at a big, rambling, white house, shaded by tall elms, and with wide piazzas on three sides. An old-fashioned flower garden, with high box-bordered beds was at the back, and broad, rolling acres, spread out on every side but one, where there was a grove of grand old trees.

The late afternoon sunlight was throwing long, level beams across the green lawn, touching everything with a golden light as they drove up to the side door, and Nan said to herself,

"I don't see how anybody could help being well and happy here."

XIV. THEODORE GIVES CARROTS A CHANCE

Theodore dreaded to go home that night. After his work was done he went to a restaurant for supper and then strolled on to the Common. It was cool and pleasant there under the wide-spreading trees, and he sat down on one of the benches and wondered what Nan was doing then and how Little Brother had borne the long hours of travel.

When it was quite dark he went slowly homeward. Mrs. Hunt's door stood open and he stopped to get the key which Nan was to leave there for him. Jimmy sprang up and brought it to him, and Mrs. Hunt gave him a kind word or two and asked him to come in and sit awhile, but he said he was tired, and taking the key, he crossed the hall and unlocked Nan's door. As he closed it behind him he gave a little start, for he saw something move over by the window. The next instant he realised that it was only Nan's chair which had rocked a little from the jar of the closing door. The room was unlighted except for the faint glimmer near the open windows.

As Theo sat down in the rocking-chair, a wave of loneliness and homesickness swept over him. Nan and Little Brother had made all the home feeling he had ever known, and never before had he felt so absolutely alone and friendless as he did to-night.

Tag seemed to share the feeling too. He went sniffing about the room, evidently searching for the two who were gone, and finally, with a long breath like a sigh, he dropped down beside the rocking-chair and rubbed his head against his master's hand with a low, troubled whine. Theodore patted the rough head as he said,

"Pretty lonesome, ain't it, old fellow?" and Tag rapped the floor with his tail and whined again.

For a long time the boy sat there gravely thinking. At last, with a sigh, he said to himself, "Might's well go to bed. Don't feel like doin' anything to-night."

He was used to undressing in the dark and he did not light the lamp, but as he was about to get into bed his hand touched something smooth and stiff that was lying on the pillow.

"It's a letter," he exclaimed, wonderingly, and he hastened to light the lamp.

"Oh!" he cried, breathlessly, as he saw the bold, firm handwriting. "It's from the bishop."

His cheeks were flushed, his eyes shining and his fingers fairly shaking with excitement as he held the letter carefully in his hands, reading and rereading the address.

"THEODORE BRYAN,

Care of MRS. MARTIN."

He thought how many times he had sat beside the bishop's desk and watched the pen travelling so rapidly across the paper. Theodore would have known that writing anywhere.

For a long time he did not open the letter. It was happiness enough to know that it was there in his hands, the first letter he had ever received. And to think that the bishop should have written it--to him, Theodore Bryan! It was a pity that the bishop could not have seen the boy's face as he stood looking with glowing eyes at the envelope.

At last he opened it and began to read the letter. It was a long one, and as the boy read on and on, his breath came quicker and his eyes grew dim, and when he had finished it his cheeks were wet, but he did not know it. He was not thinking of himself. There were many who would have given much for a letter from the bishop, but surely none could have appreciated one more than did the lonely boy who stood there that night in the dimly-lighted room poring over those closely written pages. Again and again he read the whole letter, and many times he read over one passage until the words were written in letters of light on his heart. When at last he went to bed it was to lie awake for hours with the letter held tightly in his hand, while he repeated to himself those words that he was to remember as long as he lived.

"Mrs. Martin writes me that you are anxious to be assured of my forgiveness. My dear boy, if you have ever wronged me I forgive you as freely and fully as I hope for forgiveness myself; but, Theodore, had you wronged me ever so deeply, it would all be blotted out by the joy it gives me to know that you are a soldier of the Cross. I know that you will be a faithful soldier--loyal even unto death--and may the great Captain whom we both serve, have you ever in His holy keeping."

Over and over the boy repeated these words as he lay sleepless, but full of deep happiness and peace. "Whom we both serve." The wise and holy bishop and he, a poor ignorant street boy, were soldiers now under the one great Captain. Faithful and loyal even unto death? Ah yes, Theodore pledged himself anew to such service in the watches of that night.

Nevertheless, the letter had brought to the boy a fresh disappointment, for it informed him that the bishop had been ill ever since he left the city, and that it had been decided that he should remain away until October.

"Five months longer before I can see him," Theodore thought sorrowfully, yet he could not grieve as he had done before. It almost seemed as if he could feel the bishop's hand actually resting upon his head, and see the kind eyes looking down into his. The boy had not been so happy since he left the bishop's house as he was on this night when he had expected to be so lonely and miserable.

"Oh if Nan only knew, how glad she would be," he thought more than once.

He slept at last with the letter clutched tightly in his hand, and his fingers had not loosed their hold when he awoke the next morning, nor had the joy died out of his heart. His thoughts were very busy as he dressed, and suddenly he stopped short, with one shoe on and the other in his hand.

"That's it!" he cried aloud. "That's what the bishop meant that Sunday! 'Ye are not your own. Ye are bought with a price.' The great Captain's bought me for one of His soldiers, an' I've got to do what He says. I never knew before just what that meant, but I do now." Then he added, softly, "But I want to do what He says, anyhow."

Going forth in this spirit to his work, Theodore could hardly fail to find something to do for his Captain.

Mrs. Hunt had decided to take up the work that Nan had been doing, and to furnish supplies for the stand. She had the big basket all ready when Theodore came from his room, and he and Jimmy set off with it for the stand where both the boys now took their breakfasts.

Theodore was unusually quiet and thoughtful, and there was something in his face that silenced Jimmy's lively tongue that morning. The two boys had just gotten their stand ready for business, when Theodore exclaimed, eagerly,

"There he is now!" and darted off.

Jimmy looked after him in wonder that turned to indignation, as he saw Theo lay a detaining hand on the ragged jacket of Carrots, who was slouching aimlessly along the sidewalk with his hands in his pockets, and, after a little talk with him, bring him back to the stand.

"Well now, I like that!" muttered Jimmy under his breath. He glowered darkly at Carrots as Theo drew him up to the stand, but Theodore looked into Jimmy's face with a strange light in his eyes, as he filled a plate for Carrots and poured him out a cup of coffee.

"Sh'ld think you'd better wait till he'd paid for what he jagged here that last time," Jimmy muttered, with a scowling glance at the culprit.

Carrots, overhearing the remark, grinned, and then winked impudently at Jimmy, while he disposed with all speed of the contents of the plate that Theodore had set before him. Once or twice he cast a puzzled glance at the latter as if trying to discover some hidden motive.

"Had 'nough?" Theo questioned, when plate and cup were empty.

"'Spect I might get outside of one or two o' them doughnuts," Carrots answered, with another wink at Jimmy's clouded face.

When the doughnuts also had disappeared, Theo said, "Come along a bit with me, Carrots," and the two walked off together, leaving Jimmy for the first time savagely angry with his friend Theodore.

Carrots slouched along at Theo's side, with his narrow eyes roving suspiciously from side to side in search of a possible policeman, into whose hands he suspected that his companion might be scheming to deliver him. He could not conceive the possibility of anybody's failing to avenge a wrong if he had the chance.

"Carrots," began Theodore, "where do you sleep?"

"Can't catch me that way," thought Carrots to himself, as he answered carelessly, "Oh anywheres 't I happen ter find myself when I'm sleepy."

"No reg'lar place--no home?" questioned Theo.

"Nope."

"Well, I've paid rent up to the end of the month for the room I've been sleepin' in, an' I shan't use it any more. You can sleep there for nothin' for the next week if you like."

Carrots stopped short and gazed at his companion with his tongue in his cheek.

"Think I'm a fool?" he asked, shortly.

"I do' know whether ye are or not. 'Seems to me you will be 'f ye say 'no' to my offer," and Theo looked straight into the shifty eyes of his companion.

That straightforward look puzzled Carrots. It was more convincing than any words. He studied Theo's face for a moment, then he burst out, "What's your game, anyhow, Tode Bryan?"

"Carrots," exclaimed Theo, earnestly, "there's no game at all about it. I've got the room, an' I don't need it, 'cause I've taken another one. You're welcome to use this till the month's up. Now, what d'ye say? Will ye take it or leave it?"

"I'll--take--it," rejoined Carrots, slowly.

"All right." Theo gave him the number, adding, "Come to my room anytime 'fore ten for the key."

Then he hurried on, leaving Carrots in a maze of wonder, doubt and indecision, for he could not yet believe that Theo meant honestly by him.

As for Theo, he whistled cheerily as he hastened on, for he felt that he had been doing a bit of his Captain's business. He was not in the least deceived. He knew that Carrots was a "bad lot," as he expressed it, but he said to himself, "I was a bad lot, too, not so very long ago, an' I'll see if I can't do something for Carrots while I'm a-huntin' for that Jack Finney."

Jimmy Hunt was on the lookout for Theodore that evening, and pounced upon him the moment he appeared. Jimmy's face was still clouded, and he made no response to his friend's cheery greeting. "I say, Theo," he began, "I'd like to know what you meant by it, anyhow."

"What's the trouble, Jimmy? What do you mean?"

"What d'you mean by luggin' that thievin', sarcy Carrots over t' the stand this mornin' an' stuffin' him with grub, an' never askin' him for a red cent?" Jimmy spoke in a deeply aggrieved tone.

"You won't lose anything by it, Jim. That comes out o' my share of the profits," Theo answered, quickly.

"'Tain't that," responded Jimmy, hastily. "I wouldn't 'a' minded if it had been any other feller but him. Say, Theo, what did make ye do it anyhow? Think ye might tell me that."

Theodore looked down into the face lifted to his, half curiously, half impatiently. "Jimmy," he said, gravely, "wouldn't you be glad if somebody would lend a hand to Dick and help him make a man of himself?"

Jimmy flushed. He was ashamed of his brother and mortified by Dick's evil reputation.

"'Course," he answered, shortly, dropping his eyes.

"Well, Jimmy, I'd help Dick if I could, an' there's another feller I've been huntin' for ever so long. 'Seem's if I can't find him anywheres, an' so till I do find him, I'm a-goin' to try to pull Carrots up 'stead of him."

"Pull Carrots up!" echoed Jimmy, scornfully. "Tode, you must be soft if you expect to make anything out o' such a bad lot as Carrots."

"There's a good spot in most chaps, I b'lieve, Jimmy, an' I guess there's one in Carrots, if I can only find it. Anyhow, I'm a-goin' to try for a while."

"Huh!" growled Jimmy. He said no more, but after this he watched Theo and Carrots closely, and did a deal of earnest thinking on the subject.

Carrots slept in Theodore's room for the next week--slipping softly up and down the stairs, with furtive, suspicious glances into every dark corner in the halls at night, and departing in the same fashion before Theo was up in the morning. He uttered no word of gratitude, but Theo knew better than to expect anything of that sort.

One night when he came in, Theodore sat with his door wide open, and called out pleasantly,

"Come in a minute, Carrots."

The boy paused on the threshold until he had satisfied himself that there was no one else in the room, then he sidled in and dropped heavily on a chair.

"Wal', what's wanted?" he inquired, gruffly.

"Like to earn a little extra money to-morrow?" Theodore began.

"That depends."

"Depends on what?"

"On the kind o' work."

"Well, I should think you'd be ready for any kind of work," Theodore remarked, with a quick glance at the ragged garments of the other.

Carrots grinned, carelessly. "Oh I ain't a swell like you," he replied, casting, what he meant for a scornful look at the other boy's clean outing shirt and decent suit. Theodore had reached the point now where he had at least one clean shirt a week.

He ignored the remark and went on, "There's plenty of fellers that would be glad of this job, but I want to give you the first chance at it. Jimmy Hunt's goin' on an excursion to-morrow, an' can't run the stand. You can run it if you want to."

Carrots gazed at him with mouth and eyes wide open.

"Me?" he exclaimed, incredulously. "You mean't you'll let me run it--alone-- 'thout you bossin' the job?"

Theo nodded.

Carrots' mouth slowly stretched into a grin of mingled satisfaction and derision, as he exclaimed, "All right. I'm your man!"

"Then be ready to go with me at half past six," replied Theo. Then he added, "Look here--what's your real name? Tain't Carrots I know. If you'll tell me what 'tis I'll call you by it."

"Do' want none o' yer callin'! Carrots's good 'nough for me, an' if I'm suited, other folks needn't ter interfere," growled the boy, with renewed suspicion.

"No need to get huffy 'bout it," rejoined Theodore. "It put me up a peg when folks begun to call me Theodore 'stead of Tode or Toady, an' so I thought you'd feel the same way. 'Course, if you like to be Carrots, nobody cares."

"Humph!" grunted Carrots, and departed without further discussion of the matter.

He was waiting in the hall when Theodore opened his door the next morning and assisted handily enough about carrying the big basket and arranging the stand. He did not, however, believe that Theo meant to leave him actually in charge, until he found himself established behind the neat counter with fifty cents in nickels and pennies in his pocket, to make change.

"Wal', I'm blest!" he exclaimed, and then he grinned and chuckled and slapped his sides with glee, while Theodore went off, thinking to himself,

"It's a risk, but I had to give him his chance."

Many times during that morning he thought of Carrots and wondered how he was getting on. It was a hot day and an unusually tiresome one for Theodore, and it was later than usual when he returned to his room. Before he had closed the door Jimmy Hunt ran across the hall calling out,

"Say, Theo, where's the baskets an' things?"

Theodore's heart sank, but he answered quietly, "Haven't they been brought back?"

"No. Who'd you get to run the stand, Theo?"

"Carrots."

"Theodore Bryan--you didn't!" exclaimed Jimmy, in such a tragic tone, that Theo almost laughed outright. His amusement was the last straw to Jimmy. He burst into a storm of scornful blame in the midst of which Theo quietly stepped into his room and shut the door, leaving Jimmy to fume and storm as much as he chose. That brought the boy to himself. He began to cool down and to remember, that after all, the stand belonged to Theodore, and he had a right to do as he pleased with it. So after standing in the hall, kicking at the banisters for a while, to relieve his feelings, Jimmy knocked at the closed door and in response to Theo's "come in," he went in, in a somewhat calmer state of mind.

"What you goin' to do in the mornin', Theo?" he began, in a subdued tone.

"Have you been to the stand, Jim?"

"Yes, an' that scamp after he'd sold all the stuff went to work an' auctioned off the dishes an' coffee-urn an' everything. Just skinned the place out slick," Jimmy burst out, indignantly. "I went 'round to see where the baskets was, an' some fellers told me all about it. They said 'twas a red-headed chap done it, but I couldn't b'lieve you'd be green 'nough to trust that Carrots. Say, Theo, did you re'ely think he'd do the square thing, by you?"

"Not much. I hoped he would an' I had to give him a chance, Jimmy?"

"Why'd you have to?" asked Jimmy, curiously.

"Where would I be now if somebody hadn't given me a chance, Jimmy?"

"Oh, you--you ain't Carrots. You're another sort."

"Yes, I'm another sort now, but I was bad as Carrots before I met Nan an' Little Brother," answered Theo, earnestly. Then he added, "Don't you worry 'bout the stand. I'll go out presently an' buy what's wanted."

"An' ain't ye going to do nothin' ter that Carrots for this, neither?" inquired Jimmy, anxiously.

"No, nothing. But, Jimmy, don't fret yourself about him. If he keeps on as he's been doin', he'll soon find himself locked up."

"'N' he'd oughter be too," muttered Jimmy, as he went away, leaving Theodore to think over the failure of his attempt. He was not much surprised, though he had not expected quite such a clean sweep on Carrots' part, and the loss was not heavy enough to embarrass him at all. At Mr. Scott's suggestion, Theo had begun to deposit his extra earnings in a savings bank and he had enough on hand to easily replace the dishes and utensils lost, but he was disappointed and disheartened. It seemed so useless to try to help one who would not try to help himself. And yet he could not be quite discouraged since he always remembered what he himself had once been.

He went out and bought what was needed and when he came back he found Mr. Scott just turning away from his door. He hastened to unlock it and the gentleman turned back, saying,

"I'm glad you came before I had got away, Theodore, for I want to talk over that boys' club plan with you."

"I thought you'd forgot all about it," replied the boy, his face brightening.

He had spoken to his teacher about this plan, and Mr. Scott had answered, "Yes, something of the sort may be done, but if I were in your place I wouldn't be in a hurry about it," and so the matter had been left.

Now Mr. Scott looked thoughtfully about the room, saying, "You must find this far more comfortable than the room you had before. Don't you sleep better here, Theo?"

"Oh, yes, I don't feel so tired in the morning."

"No, because you have the windows here and can have better air; but, Theo, do you realise how it would be if you should use this for a club-room? Some of the boys would be here every evening, and you'd have to have lights burning, and by the time you were ready to go to bed, the room would be very hot and stuffy--full of bad air. Besides you would have to be here all the time. You couldn't trust such boys in your room alone."

Theodore thought of Carrots, and his face was grave and disturbed as he answered, slowly, "'Spect you're right, Mr. Scott, but I do hate to give up the plan."

"Perhaps we won't give it up, only change it a little. Have you ever been in the large front room, upstairs?"

Theodore shook his head, with a look of surprise, that his teacher should know anything about the rooms upstairs.

Mr. Scott added, "Well then, suppose you come up with me now, and take a look at it. I have the key."

Wondering much, the boy followed his teacher up the stairs to a large room with two windows on each side.

"How would this do for your clubroom, Theodore?" Mr. Scott inquired.

"This? Oh, this would be fine--but Mr. Scott, it would cost a pile for this."

"Rather more than for yours, of course, but now this is the way of it, Theodore. I liked your plan about the club, but I didn't like the idea of your giving up your own room to it, so I spoke to several gentlemen of my acquaintance about the matter, and they all wanted to have a hand in it. So they each gave me a sum of money, and then I interviewed your landlord and rented this room. He is going to have it whitewashed, and then we shall have the floor thoroughly scrubbed and outside blinds put on these sunny windows. Then we shall put in some tables and chairs and some plain pine shelves for the books and papers that we are going to collect from our friends, and if you like, some of us will give the boys a talk on current events once a week or so."

"What's current events?" interposed Theo, quickly.

"You'll soon find out. Now then, Theo, we must have somebody to take charge of this room. Can you do it?"

"Yes, indeed."

"You know that means that you must be here every evening in the week, from half past seven to ten o'clock. You'll want to be away sometimes, Theodore."

"Yes, I s'pose I will, but I'm ready to stay here all the same until night school begins again."

"Very well, then we'll let it be so, and we'll try to have the room ready for our opening in a week or two--as soon as we have enough books and papers to begin with." Mr. Scott locked the door as he spoke, and the two went downstairs.

Theodore's face was full of satisfaction over the promised reading-room, but it clouded a little as his teacher said,

"You mustn't be disappointed, Theodore, if very few boys spend their evenings in this room for a while. Most of the boys in this neighbourhood are so used to loafing about the streets, that they like that best, especially in hot weather, and, of course, few of them care much for reading. They will have to be educated up to it."

"S'pose that's so," replied the boy, thoughtfully, "but they'll like it next winter when it's cold an' stormy outside," he added.

"Yes," assented the gentleman, adding, as he turned to depart, "Theo, Mrs. Rawson will be home to-morrow. Don't you want to come and take supper with us, and hear what she has to say about Nan, and the little one?"

"Oh, yes, thank you, sir," cried Theodore, with a happy smile.

"All right, then, we shall expect you," and with a pleasant "Good-night," Mr. Scott went away.

Theodore rather dreaded the supper with Mrs. Rawson, but he forgot to be shy or ill at ease when she began to tell him about the delightful old farmhouse, and the happy times that Nan and the baby were having there. She told him everything she could think of that would be of interest to him, and he listened to it all with an eager face, and a glad heart. If Little Brother must be far away from him, Theodore was happy in the assurance that the child was in such a beautiful place, and that already he had begun to grow stronger and brighter.

XV. A STRIKE

"No cars a-runnin'! What's up?" exclaimed Jimmy, the next morning, as he and Theodore passed down Tremont street.

"There's a strike on. Didn't you hear 'bout it yesterday?" replied Theo.

"No. My! But there'll be a time if all the cars stop."

"A pretty bad time--'specially for the folks that live outside the city," Theodore answered, soberly.

When, after taking his breakfast at the stand, he went back through Tremont street, groups of men and boys were standing about in every corner, and everywhere the strike was the one topic of conversation. There were groups of motormen and conductors here and there, some looking grave and anxious, and some careless and indifferent.

As the morning advanced the throngs in the streets increased. Belated business men hurried along, and clerks and saleswomen with flushed faces and anxious eyes, tried impatiently to force their way through the crowds to get to their places of business.

Theodore noticed the large number of rough-looking men and boys on the streets, and that most of them seemed full of suppressed excitement. Now and then as he passed some of these, he caught a low-spoken threat, or an exultant prophecy of lively times to come. It all made him vaguely uneasy, and he had to force himself to go about his work instead of lingering outside to see what would happen.

In one office, while he was busy over the brasses, three gentlemen were discussing the situation, and the boy, as he rubbed and polished, listened intently to what was said.

"What do the fellows want? What's their grievance, anyhow?" inquired one man, impatiently, as he flicked the ashes from his cigar.

"Shorter hours and better pay," replied a second.

184

"Of course. That's what strikers always want," put in a third. "They seem to think they're the only ones to be considered."

"Well, I must confess that I rather sympathise with the men this time," said the second speaker. "I hold that they ought to have shorter hours."

"There are plenty that will be glad enough to take their places, though."

"I suppose so, but all the same I maintain that these companies that are amply able to treat their men better, ought to do so. I believe in fair play. It pays best in the end to say nothing of the right and wrong of it."

"Think the company will give in?" questioned one.

"Guess not. I hear that the superintendent has telegraphed to New York and Chicago for men."

"There'll be trouble if they come!" exclaimed the first speaker.

"I believe," said another man, joining the group, "I believe that Sanders is responsible for all this trouble--or the most of it, anyhow. He's a disagreeable, overbearing fellow who--even when he grants a favor, which is seldom enough--does it in a mean, exasperating fashion that takes all the pleasure out of it. I had some dealings with him once, and I never want anything more to do with him. If he'd been half-way decent to the men there would never have been any strike, in my opinion."

Sanders was the superintendent of the road where the trouble was.

"You're right about Sanders," said another. "I always have wondered how he could keep his position. These strikes though, never seem to me to do any real good to the cause of the strikers, and a great many of the men realise that too, but these walking delegate fellows get 'round 'em and persuade 'em that a strike is going to end all their troubles--and so it goes. I saw that little sneak--Tom Steel--buttonholing the motormen, and cramming them with his lies, as I came along just now. There's always mischief where Tom Steel is."

By this time Theodore had finished his work, and he left the office, his head full of strikes, superintendents, and walking delegates, and wherever he went that day, the strike was the only subject discussed.

He stopped work earlier than usual, finding himself infected with the prevailing unrest and excitement. He found the sidewalks of the principal business streets thronged with men, women and boys, all pressing in one direction.

"Come along, Tode!" cried a shrill voice at his elbow, and he turned to find Jimmy Hunt, his round face all alight with anticipation of exciting episodes to follow. Jimmy began talking rapidly.

"They've been smashin' cars, Tode, an' haulin' off the motormen an' conductors that want to keep on workin'. There's three cars all smashed up near the sheds, an' the strikers say they'll wreck every one that's run out to-day."

"It's a shame!" declared Theo, indignantly; yet boy-like, if there was to be a mob fight, he wanted to be on hand and see it all, and he took care not to let Jimmy get far ahead of him.

As they went on, the crowd continually increased until it became so dense that the boys had to worm their way through it inch by inch. They pressed on, however, and when further progress was impossible, they found standing room on the very front close to the car-track.

It had been a noisy, blustering crowd as it surged along the street, but now that it had come to a standstill, a sudden breathless silence fell upon it, and all eyes turned in one direction, gazing eagerly, intently up the track. Suddenly, a low, hoarse cry broke from a hundred throats.

"It's comin'! It's comin'!" and far up the street a car appeared.

The faces of the men grew more hard and determined. Those of the women became pale and terrified. The two boys peered eagerly forward, their hearts beating quickly, with dread mingled with a sort of wild excitement.

"Look, Theo--Look!" whispered Jimmy, pointing to some men who were hastily digging up cobble-stones from the street. "There's Carrots, too," he added.

"Wonder who that little chap is--the one that seems to have so much to say to the car men," Theo replied, thoughtfully.

"That's Tom Steel. You've heard of him, hain't ye?" A man at Theo's elbow was speaking. "He's responsible for this strike, I think, an' I hope he'll get his pay for it too," he added, grimly.

Theodore glanced up into the grave face of the speaker and recognised him as a motorman. Evidently, he was more bitter against the strikers than against the company.

The car was now close at hand, and all at once as with a single impulse, there was a surging forward, and the crowd closed in blocking the track with a solid mass of human beings. The motorman set his teeth hard, and rang the gong loudly, insistently. The conductor hastened through the car and stood beside him. The only passenger was a policeman, who stood on the rear platform calmly gazing at the sea of angry, excited faces on either side.

"This car's got to stop!" shouted a big, brawny fellow, springing onto the step and giving the motorman a threatening glance.

"This car ain't a-goin' to stop!" retorted the motorman, grimly, as he released the brake.

"We'll see about that," and with the words the big fellow seized the man's arms and wrenched his hand off the lever.

The conductor sprang to the assistance of his comrade while the policeman ran forward and pushed the man roughly off the car.

In the same instant, Theo saw Carrots snatch a box from a bootblack near him and with a wild yell of defiance, hurl it through one of the car windows. The shrill, taunting cry of the boy, mingled with the crash of the breaking glass, and the sight of the policeman's upraised club, aroused the mob to sudden fury. At once there arose a wild hubbub of shouts, yells and cries, followed by a shower of cobble-stones, and a fierce rush upon the three men on the car, and in two minutes the car was a shattered wreck; the motorman and conductor were being hustled through the crowd with threats and warnings, while the policeman's club had been wrenched from his grasp. He drew his pistol, but with a howl of fury it was knocked from his hand, and the next moment he lay senseless upon the ground, felled by a savage blow from his own club.

The taste of conflict, the sight of blood, had roused to a fierce flame the smouldering spirit of lawlessness and insurrection in the mob. A savage rage seemed to have taken possession of the men as, with frantic haste and mad delight, they tore up cobble-stones and built a huge barricade across the track. When it was completed, Carrots darted up on top of it and waved a red handkerchief above his head. A hoarse roar of approval broke from the mob, but Steel sternly ordered the boy down and hissed in his ear,

"You fool! You might have spoiled everything by that! Don't ye show that again till I give the signal--d'ye hear?"

Carrots nodded with an evil gleam in his narrow eyes, that made Theo shiver.

"Come on, now. We've done enough for once," Steel added, and keeping his hand on the arm of the boy the two disappeared in the throng that was slowly melting away.

Then, with a long breath, Jimmy turned to Theodore.

"My!" he exclaimed, in a tone of shuddering satisfaction. "It's awful, ain't it, Theo! S'pose he's dead?" He gazed with half fearful interest toward the policeman who had been clubbed and about whom a group had gathered.

"Looks like it. There comes some more p'lice. They'll take care of him. Come on, Jimmy, le's go home."

188

"Oh, no, Theo, don't go home, yet. Le's go an' see what's goin' on over there," and Jimmy turned into a cross street through which the greater portion of the crowd was pressing.

"There's something the matter over at the depot," said Theodore, as he followed, half willingly and half reluctantly, in Jimmy's eager footsteps.

About the depot there was usually a constant stream of cars coming and going, but to-day the streets looked bare and deserted.

When the boys reached the square only two cars were in sight and these two were approaching, one behind the other, on the same track. As they drew near, they were seen to contain each six or eight policemen, fully armed and with stern, resolute faces. The mob again howled and hooted at the motormen and conductors, and showered them with dirt and small stones, but made no attempt to stop the cars.

No cars were run after dark that evening, and the next day they were run only at intervals of an hour and each one carried a heavily armed guard. The strikers and their lawless sympathisers continued to throng the streets and to threaten all car-men who remained on duty. Now and then a car window was broken or an obstruction placed on the tracks, but there was no serious outbreak, and it was rumoured that a compromise between the company and the strikers was under consideration and that the trouble would soon be at an end.

So a week slipped away. One morning Theodore was on his way from one office to another when he heard the sound of drum and fife and saw a body of the strikers marching up Washington street. Every boy within sight or hearing at once turned in after the procession, and Theodore followed with the rest.

It was about ten o'clock in the morning and the streets were full of shoppers, many of them ladies who had been afraid to venture out during the past week.

As if they had risen out of the ground, scores of rough-looking men and street boys began to push and jostle the shoppers on the narrow sidewalks until many of the frightened women took refuge in the stores, and the shopkeepers, fearful of what might follow, began hastily putting up their shutters and making ready to close their stores, if necessary. These signs of apprehension gave great delight to the rougher element in the streets, and they yelled and hooted uproariously at the cautious shopkeepers, but they did not stop. Steadily, swiftly they followed that body of men marching with dark, determined faces to the sound of the fife and the drum.

"Where are they going?" Theo asked of a man at his side and the reply was,

"To the car-house, I reckon. They're ripe for mischief now."

"What's stirred 'em up again--anything new?" the boy questioned.

"Many of the strikers have been discharged and new men brought on--five hundred of them--from New York and Chicago. I'm afraid we haven't seen the worst of the troubles yet."

"Look! Look!" cried a boy, close beside Theodore, and the latter looking ahead, saw a squad of mounted officers coming through a cross street. Without stopping to parley they charged into the marching strikers and dispersed them, silencing the fife and drum, and when the furious mob of followers and sympathisers yelled threats and defiance at the officers, the latter charged into the mob riding up to the pavement and forcing the people back into the stores and dwellings behind them.

This was as fuel to the fire of anger and insurrection. Deep and dire threats passed from lip to lip, and evil purpose hardened into grim determination as the mob slowly surged in the direction of the car-house, after the officers had passed on. The throng was far more quiet now, and far more dangerous. Again and again, Theodore caught glimpses of Tom Steel's insignificant face, and like a long, dark shadow, Carrots followed ever at his heels.

No cars were running now, but the boy heard low-spoken references to new men and "scabs," and "the will of the people," as, almost without effort of his own, he was borne onward with the throng.

At a little distance from the car-house the strikers again drew together and stood mostly in gloomy silence, their eyes ever turning toward the closed doors of the great building before them. The vast crowd waited, too, in a silence that seemed to throb and pulse with intense and bitter feeling. The strikers had stopped in the middle of the street, and around them on every side, except toward the car-house, the crowd pressed and surged like a vast human sea. There were not many women in the number gathered there, and the few who were there were of the lowest sort, but men and boys--largely tramps, roughs and street boys--were there in countless numbers, mingled with not a few of the better class.

Slowly the minutes passed, until an hour had gone by, and it began to be whispered about that the company dared not run any cars. Still the men waited, and the crowd waited too. But at last some grew weary of inaction, and when Steel proposed that they spend the time barricading the tracks, his suggestion met with a quick response.

From a neighbouring street the men brought Belgian blocks and piled them on the track. They pulled down tree boxes and broke off branches of trees, and when an ice wagon came along they took possession of the huge blocks of ice and capped their barricade with these.

Suddenly the doors of the car-house were thrown open, and a car rolled slowly out.

There was an instant of breathless silence, followed by a roar like that of a thousand savage beasts, as the strikers saw that new men were running the car, and that it carried half a score of policemen, armed to the teeth.

As it approached the barricade some of the officers sprang off and began to throw down the obstructions, the others standing ready to fire upon the mob if necessary. The crowd showered bitter words and taunts upon the officers, but did not venture to molest them. The motorman stood with his hand on the lever, ready to start the car the moment the track should be clear. Carrots, with a pack of street Arabs at his heels, jeered at the new motorman, climbing up on the car and taunting him, until, at last, his patience was exhausted, and he suddenly lifted his foot and kicked one of the boys off the car. The boy fell heavily to the ground, and instantly the shrill voice of Carrots was uplifted, crying frantically,

"He's killed Billy Green! He's killed Billy Green! Pitch in to him, boys! Pitch into him!"

Billy Green was already picking himself up, with no worse injury than a cut in his cheek, but the mob took up the cry, and,

"Pitch into him! Pitch into him! Kill him! Kill him!" was shouted by hundreds of savage voices as the crowd pressed about the car. They tried to drag the motorman off, in spite of the guards, they smashed the car windows, they tore out the cushions, they beat the policemen, and wrenched their clubs out of their hands. Finally several of the officers drew their pistols and fired into the air.

At this the crowd fell back for a second, and the turmoil of shouts and cries that had been deafening a moment before, died away in sudden silence--a threatening, dangerous silence as of a wild beast about to spring.

Into this instant of silence broke a new cry from the outskirts of the crowd.

"It's the mayor. Make way for the mayor!"

"No, it's the bishop. Make way for the bishop! Stand back! Stand back!"

At this cry, Theodore turned like a flash and gazed in the direction in which all eyes were turning. There was no mistake. The bishop was surely one of the occupants of a carriage that was slowly forcing its way through the throng.

With his heart beating with a wild joy; his eyes glowing; the colour coming and going in his cheeks, Theodore stood still until the carriage stopped.

Then sliding through the smallest spaces, darting between feet, this way and that, the boy managed somehow to reach the side of the carriage, where he stood with his hand on one of the wheels, his eager, burning gaze fastened on the face he loved so well. Instinctively he pulled off his cap, but he made no attempt to attract the attention of the bishop. He uttered no word or sound. He only stood with all his loving heart in his eyes, and looked.

The bishop's expression was very grave, as he gazed over that vast sea of faces. He turned to speak to the gentleman who sat beside him, and as he did so, his eyes fell on Theodore's eloquent upturned countenance. A quick, bright smile flashed across his face, and reaching down, he laid his hand for a moment gently upon the boy's bared head.

Before he could speak the silence was again broken by a cry from many lips--a cry of warning now, rather than a threat, though again the words were,

"Stop the car! Stop the car! The bishop! The bishop!"

The bishop's carriage had come to a standstill directly across the track, the crowd being here so dense that it was impossible for the driver to go even a yard farther.

The policemen had cleared the barricade from the track, and then sprung hastily on the car again. Evidently they had not noticed the dangerous position of the carriage, and now the motorman started the car forward. The man was a stranger in the city. He knew nothing about the bishop--cared nothing about him. He was there to run that car, and he meant to do it or die in the attempt, so when the crowd shouted,

"The bishop! The bishop!" he yelled in reply,

"Get out of the way then if you don't want him hurt. This car's a-going through, bishop or no bishop!"

The car was already in motion. The crowd pushed and struggled and tried to fall back and let the carriage pass over the track, but it was impossible, so closely were the people packed together there.

On the car came, while for an instant the crowd waited with tense breath for what should follow.

"Loyal unto death." The words rang through Theodore's brain, as in that instant he sprang swiftly forward and flung himself across the track directly in front of the slowly moving car. A cry of horror broke from the throng and a score of hands were stretched forth to draw the boy from his dangerous position, but he clung to the fender and would not be removed.

"Stop the car!" he pleaded. "Oh stop the car or the bishop will be killed!"

Never a thought of his own danger had the boy,--for he would have given his young life freely and joyfully for his bishop, but the sacrifice was not needed. The police, now seeing the danger, forced the furious motorman to stop the car until the crowd had had time to fall back and the carriage had safely crossed the track. Then the car passed on followed by threatening glances and menacing words from the angry throng.

But now the bishop arose in the carriage, and as he stood in the majesty of his great height with the light of a pure heart and a holy life illumining his face--once again a hush fell upon that vast gathering, and when the rich voice rolled out upon the still air, uttering its message of heavenly love, and strong, sweet counsels of peace and justice, the hearts of the people were melted within them. Hard, brutal men and rude street boys listened, feeling a strange power that they could not understand, thrilling their souls, and compelling them, in spite of their own wills, to follow the counsels of this servant of God.

No other man in that great city was honoured and loved by rich and poor alike, as was the bishop. To no other would such a crowd in such a mood have hearkened, but they stood in silence and listened breathlessly as if they feared to lose a single word. They listened as if they knew that never again would such a message come to them from those lips. Stern, bitter faces softened, and hard eyes dimmed with tears as the burning, melting words fell on the listening ears. Women wept, and men forgot their hatreds and their grievances. Only here and there an evil face grew more evil as the bishop's words worked upon the hearts and consciences of that vast throng.

Tom Steel dropped his mask of careless indifference, as he tried to stem the tide by whispering sneers and taunts to one and another, but they would have none of his counsels now, and after a while he slunk away with a black scowl on his face and evil words on his lips, and still beside him slouched the gaunt, ragged figure with its crown of rough red hair; and no one bade them stay; no one listened to their wicked whispers, for the bishop's words were filling every ear and every heart.

At last, the bishop stretched forth his hands and pronounced a tender blessing upon them all, and then he drove slowly away, and when he was gone rough men looked into each other's faces, half wondering, half ashamed, as they moved away. They had no desire now for rioting and lawlessness--for deeds of blood and violence. The Spirit of God had touched their hearts. The atmosphere in which the bishop lived and moved and had his being had for the time enveloped even these. No wonder then, that it had wrought such a transformation in the heart and life of one little street boy.

That same night two hundred of the city clergymen united in an appeal to the company to submit the troubles to arbitration, and to this both the company and the strikers agreed. The result was that although all that the men asked was not granted, yet their hours were shortened, and an increase of pay promised at the beginning of the year.

XVI. CALLED TO GO UP HIGHER

As for Theodore--when the bishop's carriage had driven away he went home in a state of joyous expectation. He thought how he would go, on the morrow, to the bishop's house, and of the long talk they two would have together, when he would tell his friend all that he had so often longed to tell him. He knew well how interested the bishop would be in all that he-- Theodore--was trying to do for the Great Captain, and he longed to talk over his work and his plans with one so wise and so experienced.

On his way home he stopped and bought some linen collars and cuffs and a neat necktie.

"'Cause I want to look as well's I can when he sees me," he said to himself.

All that evening he thought of that visit which he would make the next day. He realty could not wait any longer, but he found it hard to decide what would be the best hour for him to go. He knew that the bishop was very often away in the evening, or if at home he was almost sure to have guests with him. In the afternoon, too, he seldom had a leisure moment. Indeed he never had any leisure moments, but Theodore decided at last that the best time to see him would be between twelve and one o'clock.

All night, in his dreams, he saw himself making his way to the house and once he awoke in great distress, imagining that Brown had sternly refused him admittance.

He could not work that next morning, but he wanted somebody else to share his happiness, and so to all the sick and shut-in ones in the two houses, he carried some little gift. It was his thank-offering, though he did not know it. Small gifts they were, all--a flower to one, a newspaper to another, some oranges to a sick woman, an extra loaf to a hard-working mother--little things all, but given in the name of the Great Captain though His Name was not once mentioned.

So, many kindly thoughts followed the boy when, at noon, he went once more through the streets toward the bishop's house.

Theodore's face had little of beauty, but the glance of his grey eyes was honest and true. He was able now to possess two suits and he wore his best one with the clean linen and the new tie. Many a mother might have been proud that day to call this boy of the streets, her son.

The remembrance of his dreams sent a shiver over Theodore as he rang the bell at the bishop's door, but Brown did not refuse him admittance. On the contrary he smiled faintly and held open the door as he said, in a low tone, "Come to Mrs. Martin's room," and once again Theodore followed him across the wide hall.

Mrs. Martin gave him a cordial welcome, but a great dread fell upon the boy as he noted her red eyes and subdued manner, and when she said,

"He talked about you last evening, Theodore, and told us what you did for him. You've come to ask how he is, haven't you?" the boy's heart sank and he dropped into the nearest chair with his eyes fixed entreatingly on the housekeeper's face. His throat felt dry and stiff, and he dared not trust himself to speak. Mrs. Martin too, sat down and wiped her eyes as she went on,

"He ought not to have gone out to speak to those strikers yesterday. He wasn't well enough, and I told the gentlemen so when they came for him, but as soon as he heard what they wanted he said he would go. He came home all tired out, and he was taken sick in the night."

Theodore tried in vain to frame a question with his trembling lips. The housekeeper guessed what he would have asked and answered as if he had spoken.

"It's some heart trouble and the doctors say he cannot live."

At these words, Theodore's head went down on the table and he sat as if stunned. His trouble seemed to him too great even for belief. Eight months before it had seemed terrible to him to know that the width of the continent separated him from his friend. Now, what a joy it would have been to him to know that the bishop was alive and well in California.

At last he lifted his head and asked in a low voice,

"How long?"

Mrs. Martin understood. She answered, sadly, "A few days--possibly only a few hours. He lies as if he were asleep, but it is not sleep. I think," she added, with a glance at the boy's heart-broken face, "I think you can see him for a moment if you would like to."

Theodore nodded and the housekeeper added, "Come then," and led the way to an upper room.

The boy followed with such an aching heart as he had never imagined that a boy could have.

The sick room was darkened and a nurse sat by the bedside. Theodore stood for a moment looking down on the face so dear to him, and so changed even in the few hours since last he saw it. He longed to press his lips to the hand that lay outstretched on the white coverlet, but he did not dare, and after a moment he turned and left the room in silence.

Mrs. Martin followed him down the stairs. At the door he stopped and looked at her, tried to speak but could not, and so went away without a word. He knew that never again should he see his friend alive, and he did not. Before the next night, the bishop had been called to go up higher.

When the announcement of his death appeared in the papers there was a request that no flowers be sent. Theodore did not notice this item, and so on the day of the funeral he carried to the house some of the roses that he knew the bishop had loved most, and Mrs. Martin herself placed them in the cold hand that a few days before, had been laid upon Theodore's head. All the gold of the earth, had it been offered to the boy, could not have purchased from him the sweet memory of that last look and touch.

On the day of the funeral, the church where the service was held was crowded, and the streets without were filled with a throng as vast as that to which so short a time before, the bishop had spoken, but what a difference was there in look and manner between the two great gatherings! Here, every face was softened, every heart tender with grief. They called him "our bishop," and they felt that they had lost one who loved them--one who was indeed their friend.

But not one, whether within or without the church, not one grieved more deeply for the grand, beautiful life so suddenly cut off than did the lad who stood without and listened to the solemn tones of the great organ, and watched with eyes dim with tears as the black-draped coffin was borne out to its burial. The boy stood there until the last of the long line of carriages had passed him; then he stepped forward and, alone and on foot, he followed to the cemetery.

When all was over, he went sorrowfully homeward, feeling as if there was a great blank in his life--a blank that could never be filled; that the world could never again seem bright to him; but that evening Mr. Scott came, and his affectionate sympathy comforted the boy's sore heart. His teacher made him feel that now, more than ever, he must be "the bishop's shadow." To Theodore, his small ministries to the forlorn and suffering ones about him, seemed, indeed, as nothing when he recalled the wide-reaching labours of the bishop, but as the days went on these small ministries grew to be the joy of his life.

Mr. Scott, watching him closely, saw how week by week he became more unselfish and thoughtful for others; more eager to help any who needed his help. It was a grief to the boy that one whom he most longed to help seemed for a time beyond his reach, and this was Carrots.

Four of the ringleaders in the riotous proceedings of the strike had been arrested, tried and sentenced to two years in the penitentiary. Of this number were Tom Steel, and Carrots, whose red banner had more than once caught the eye of the police.

Jimmy Hunt openly rejoiced, feeling that Carrots had got his deserts at last, but Theodore was troubled and disheartened over the matter. He went to see the boy in prison, and found him as gruff and surly as ever, yet he was sure that, when he came away, the eyes of Carrots followed him wistfully.

He did not go again to the prison but, though he was no more fond of letter-writing than are most boys of fourteen, yet, during those two years of Carrots' imprisonment, never a month passed in which he did not receive a long, cheery letter from Theodore. He never replied to any of these letters, but as Theodore expected no replies, that made no difference.

XVII. FINAL GLIMPSES

As the evenings lengthened, the club grew in favour among the boys of the neighbourhood, and often Mr. Scott wondered to see how Theodore succeeded in maintaining good order and in keeping up the interest of the boys, without setting them against him. He was full of ingenious ideas for interesting them in something helpful, and, as he expressed it, "lifting 'em up a peg." He grew to be exceedingly popular in the neighbourhood that winter, but he never discovered the fact. He was too busy thinking of and for others, to think much about himself.

After a while he gave up all interest in his stand to Jimmy Hunt and devoted himself wholly to his brass-polishing business. It outgrew his own time and strength before the New Year, and then he hired boys to work for him, and he spent his time superintending their work and extending his list of employers. He paid the boys as liberally as he could, but he would tolerate no loafing or careless work, so that at first he had some trouble in getting satisfactory assistants, but once secured, they seldom left his employ. The time came when he had a long list of such employees, and when a large part of the brass work in the city was under his care--but this was later.

Nan and Little Brother did not come back to the city in the fall. Mr. Scott had never intended that they should if he could prevent it.

Long before the summer was over, Nan had taken a daughter's place in Mrs. Hyde's childless home and Little Brother had become the cherished pet of the household. So warm and deep was the love given to them both that even Nan's sensitive pride could not object to remaining there where she knew that she could give as much as she received in love and service, and with a glad and grateful heart she abandoned all thought of returning to the city, and knew that she had at last found a real home.

But she did not forget her older friend, Theodore, and she told her new friends so much about him that they desired to see and know him also. So it came about that one of her letters to him contained a cordial invitation from Mrs. Hyde for him to spend Thanksgiving week at her home.

Mr. Scott gladly agreed to attend to the club-room and to keep an eye on the polishing business as far as he could, so Theodore accepted the invitation and began to look forward with delight to seeing Little Brother and Nan again.

He could hardly realise that it was he himself--poor Theodore Bryan--who, one bright November morning, sat in the swift-flying car and looked out on the autumn landscape on his way to spend Thanksgiving as Mrs. Hyde's guest, and to see again the two whom he loved to call his "folks."

As the train drew near the station at which he was to stop, Theo wondered who would meet him. He hoped Nan would. Indeed, he felt sure that she would, for, of course, Mrs. Hyde would not know him any more than he would know her. So, as the cars ran along by the platform, he gazed eagerly out of the car window, and he felt a little chill of disappointment because Nan was nowhere in sight. There was a comfortable carriage in waiting for somebody. He thought that it might be Mrs. Hyde's--but no, that could not be, either, for a big, rosy-cheeked laddie, with mischievous blue eyes, sat on the seat, flourishing a whip in true boyish fashion. That didn't look much like heavy-eyed, white-lipped Little Brother, and there was not a girl anywhere in sight, except a tall, handsome one in a beautiful grey suit, trimmed with fur. This girl stood near the carriage and seemed to be watching for some one.

"I do wish Nan had come to meet me," Theo thought, as he stepped off the train, and then the tall girl in the grey suit was looking eagerly into his face, with both hands outstretched, crying,

"Oh, Theo! How glad I am to see you!" and he was seated in the carriage with that rosy-cheeked, merry-faced little laddie, between him and Nan, before he fairly realised that this was Little Brother, grown well and strong, as even Nan had not dared hope he would do in so few months.

And he had not forgotten his old friend either--Little Brother had not,--or, if he had, he renewed the friendship very speedily, and during Theo's stay the two were as inseparable as of old.

It was a happy week for Nan, for she could see how Theodore had been growing in the best ways during the months of their separation, and she was not a bit disappointed in him, but proud to have her new friends know him. And, as for the boy, it was a glimpse into a new life for him--that week in a lovely Christian home. He made up his mind that, sometime, he would have just such a home of his own, and he went back to the city well content to leave these two in such tender hands and amid such delightful surroundings.

Through all the winter that followed, Theodore was busy and happy. When the night-school began, he coaxed Mr. Hunt to take charge of the clubroom, for Theodore wanted to learn and fit himself for better work by and by, and with such a purpose he made rapid progress in his studies.

But, busy as he was, he still found time for his Saturday evening work for the florist, that he might continue his Sunday flower mission, for he knew that those few blossoms were all of brightness and beauty that ever entered into some of those shut-in, poverty-pinched lives about him.

Then, at Christmas time, Mr. Scott and Mrs. Rawson and the King's Daughters Circle helped him prepare a Christmas tree in the clubroom; a tree that bore a gift for every child and woman in the two houses. The children almost went wild over that, the first Christmas tree that many of them had ever seen; and then the eleven girls in their pretty winter dresses served all the company with cake and cream.

Theodore was too happy and busy to eat his share, but that was all right, for Teddy Hunt had no trouble at all in disposing of two portions.

When the last candle had ceased to glimmer among the green branches, and the last bit of cake and spoonful of cream had disappeared, the company slowly and lingeringly departed, already looking forward to just such another Christmas three hundred and sixty-five days later. Then with many a "Merry Christmas" to Theodore, the girls and Mrs. Rawson took their departure, and Mr. Scott followed them, only stopping a moment, to say,

"We left your Christmas gift in your room, my boy. I hope you will like it."

Wondering what his gift might be, the boy put out the lights and locked the clubroom door and hurried down to his room, remembering then that his teacher had asked for his key earlier in the evening.

The key was in the door now, and there was a light in the room. Theodore pushed open the door and then stopped short with a cry of delighted surprise, for he never would have recognised this as the bare little room he had left.

A neat rug covered the floor, fresh shades hung at the windows; a white iron bedstead with fluffy mattress and fresh white bedding stood where the old bedstead had been, and in place of the pine table and chairs were a neat oak bureau, and a washstand with toilet set and towels, three good, comfortable chairs and a desk that made Theo's eyes shine with delight. But best of all was a picture that hung on the wall facing the door--a picture of the bishop with that tender look in the eyes that the boy remembered so well.

On a card, slipped in the corner of the frame, was written,

"From Nan and Little Brother," and Theodore, as he looked and looked, felt that there was nothing left for him to desire.

He was still standing in the middle of the floor, gazing at the picture, when there was a knock at the door and as he opened it in flocked the eleven girls with Mrs. Rawson and Mr. Scott behind them.

"Do you like it, Theodore?"

"We couldn't go home till we saw you here," they exclaimed, and laughed and chattered joyously when they saw that the boy was too pleased and delighted for any words, and then they went away with their own hearts full of the joy of giving, to write a circular letter to Nan telling her all about it.

After this the winter passed quietly to Theodore. He was well and strong, and he was busy day and evening, and he was as happy a boy as could be found in all that city.

And the weeks and months slipped away until two years had gone by, and it was time for Carrots to be released.

Theodore ascertained the day and hour when he would leave the penitentiary and met him at the very gate with a warm and friendly greeting, and took him at once to his own room.

He searched the pale face of the boy, wondering whether there really was in it a change for the better, or not. It seemed to him less sullen and more thoughtful than it had been two years before, but he was not sure. Certainly, Carrots was very quiet. It seemed almost as if he had forgotten how to talk. He looked about Theo's neat, comfortable room, evidently noting the changes there, but he made no comment.

Theodore had set out a table with a good supper for the two, and Carrots ate as if he enjoyed the food. When the meal was ended, he leaned back in his chair, and as he looked straight into Theodore's eyes, said slowly,

"What made ye do it, Tode?"

"Do what--bring you here to supper?"

"Yes, an' write all them letters to me, an'--an' everything?"

"Why, Carrots, it's this way. I served another fellow an' awful mean trick once, and I've been trying mighty hard to find him, and make it up to him, but I haven't found him yet, and so I've tried to do a little for you instead of him--don't you see?"

Carrots nodded, and Theo fancied that he looked a little disappointed.

"Then 'twasn't really me you wanted to help?" he said, gravely.

"Yes, 'twas, too," answered Theo, quickly. "I'd have done what I could for you, anyhow, Carrots, but I do wish I could find him," he added, sorrowfully.

"What's his name?" inquired Carrots.

"Jack Finney."

"What?" exclaimed the boy, staring at Theodore as if he could not believe his ears.

"Jack Finney," repeated Theo, wonderingly.

"Well, I never! Tode--I'm Jack Finney."

"You?" cried Theodore, starting up excitedly. "You Mrs. Russell's Jack Finney?"

The boy nodded again. "I guess so. I was in her class in the mission school."
Theo's face was all alight as he exclaimed, "Oh, Carrots--no, Jack, I'll never call you Carrots again--Jack, I'm too glad for anything! And now look here, Jack Finney, you've got to be the right kind of a chap from this on. I won't let you go wrong. I can't let you go wrong, Jack. It--it seems as if it'll be all my fault if you do."

And Jack, looking again straight into Theodore's eyes, answered slowly, "I guess I've had 'bout enough o' crooked doin's. If you'll stand by me, I'll make a try on the other line, anyhow."

"I'll stand by you every time, Jack," cried Theodore, earnestly.

And he did, through months of alternate hope and discouragement, for Jack did not find the upward road an easy one.

There were the bad habits of years always pulling him down, and there were old companions in evil ever ready to coax him back to their company, and more than once they succeeded for a while; but Theodore would not give him up, and in the end, the boy had his reward, for Jack Finney became his fellow-soldier under the Great Captain, and his faithful helper in his loving ministry among Christ's little ones.

Milton Keynes UK
Ingram Content Group UK Ltd.
UKHW010748180923
428890UK00004B/240